Now was the moment.

She would pull out her phone, bring up the ride app. Bid him good-night. If she did this, the past three hours could be bundled into a box neither of them would ever have to open again. He might smile at her secretively every now and then. Wink at her in acknowledgment, but that would be the end of it.

If she left now.

"Come up," he said.

It wasn't a question. It wasn't even an invitation.

It was an answer.

An answer to her own admission in the elevator. That she liked looking at him. That she could look at him more.

That he wanted her to.

"Okay," she said.

* * *

Secret Lives After Hours by Cynthia St. Aubin
is part of The Kane Heirs series.

Dear Reader,

What is it about playboys, anyway? Is it the devil-may-care attitude? The passionate pursuit of pleasure in all its forms? Or the prospect that maybe, if you play your cards right, they might just take *you* along for the ride? For me, Mason Kane is all of these with hot fudge and a cherry on top.

When he first appeared on the page in *Corner Office Confessions*, I quickly realized I had a problem. Here he was, a work-shirking, praise-stealing, shameless Casanova, and yet he insisted on being so...so... *likeable*.

No wonder then that smart, shy executive assistant Charlotte Westbrook began developing a terminal crush. But the more I got to know these two, the more apparent it became that they had much more in common than I'd originally thought. Namely, secret extracurricular pursuits outside the Kane Foods corporate headquarters that would set them on a collision course with passion...and each other.

I sincerely hope you enjoy *Secret Lives After Hours*, book two in The Kane Heirs series, and I would love it if you come find me on Facebook, TikTok or Instagram to say hello!

Sweet reading!

Cynthia

CYNTHIA ST. AUBIN

——

SECRET LIVES AFTER HOURS

HARLEQUIN

DESIRE

DESIRE

Recycling programs for this product may not exist in your area.

ISBN-13: 978-1-335-58137-2

Secret Lives After Hours

For questions and comments about the quality of this book, please contact us at CustomerService@Harlequin.com.

Harlequin Enterprises ULC
22 Adelaide St. West, 41st Floor
Toronto, Ontario M5H 4E3, Canada
www.Harlequin.com

Printed in U.S.A.

Cynthia St. Aubin wrote her first play at age eight and made her brothers perform it for the admission price of gum wrappers. When she was tall enough to reach the top drawer of her parents' dresser, she began pilfering her mother's secret stash of romance novels and has been in love with love ever since. A confirmed cheese addict, she lives in Texas with a handsome musician.

Books by Cynthia St. Aubin

The Kane Heirs

Corner Office Confessions
Secret Lives After Hours

Visit her Author Profile page at Harlequin.com, or www.cynthiastaubin.com, for more titles.

You can also find Cynthia St. Aubin on Facebook, along with other Harlequin Desire authors, at Facebook.com/harlequindesireauthors!

For aspiring authors everywhere,
quietly putting words on the page,
alternatively terrified and elated by the prospect
of anyone else ever reading them.

This is your sign.

Keep going.

Acknowledgments

Sincere and emphatic gratitude to my
talented editor, Charles Griemsman,
and my amazing agent lady, Christine Witthohn,
for their continuing encouragement and support.

My eternal thanks to my Emotional Support Human
and critique partner, Kerrigan Byrne,
for talking me off literary ledges and for the
morning TikTok avalanches that preserved
my sanity during the writing of this book.

My heartfelt appreciation goes out to the readers,
who make it possible for me to do what I love.
I wish I could send you all the snack of
your choice and a basket of kittens.

Finally, I remain ever thankful for my husband,
Ted, who is my North Star and my very own hero.
My happily-ever-after begins and ends with you.

One

Mason Kane couldn't help himself.

Not that he'd been trying very hard.

Sitting through what felt like an endless executive meeting in the twenty-fifth-floor boardroom with sprawling views of downtown Philadelphia, his dire need for distraction found an irresistible target.

Charlotte Westbrook, his father's executive assistant.

He had strategically positioned himself across from her at a table longer and wider than some swimming pools and with a surface just as glossy. There, from his carefully selected seat, he caught her stealing glances at him every time she thought his attention was focused elsewhere.

And when he did, her delicately freckled cheeks flushed a cotton-candy pink that made his heart beat a little faster behind the fabric of his tailored shirt.

He wasn't sure if it was his position as chief marketing officer at a confectionary company that inclined him to think of her in terms meant to be tasted.

Savored.

Her hair the intoxicating garnet of a good cabernet. Eyes like melted Belgian chocolate. Lips a decadent candy-apple red. Her skin pale and rosy as peaches and cream.

This combination alone had been sufficient to motivate him to quietly appreciate her through the glass wall of his office on occasion.

But now he had additional motivation.

A few months past, Mason had been handed a tidbit of information from Arlie Banks—now engaged to his twin brother, Samuel—that had buzzed around his brain like a bluebottle fly ever since.

Charlotte had a thing for him.

He'd thought the idea ridiculous at first. As far as he could remember, she had never even willingly made eye contact.

At which point Arlie had pointed out that this was actually the *chief* sign of attraction in shy girls.

Shy girls.

Mason's usual type was, well, decidedly *not* shy. Women who knew what they wanted, and what they wanted most often was to plant the red soles of their Louboutin heels on the beige ceiling of Mason's Aston Martin.

Which he had absolutely no problem with as a rule.

But a shy girl?

He didn't even know how one of those worked. How the hell Arlie had picked up on this completely baffled him when Charlotte had never—to Mason's knowledge—voluntarily spoken five words to him in a row.

Until he started looking for himself.

The longer he looked, the more he saw. The way her spine straightened every time he walked by her desk. The way her eyes, half-hidden behind the reflective lenses of her naughty-librarian glasses, always flicked up to his for a mere split second before fastening onto the screen of her monitor. The nervous way she would reach up to tuck a nonexistent hair back into the ever-present bun at the nape of her graceful neck.

Once he knew what to look for, he began seeing which of her tells he could trigger and by what means. It had started out as an experiment.

Now it had become a game.

He liked games.

A little too much sometimes.

"Mason." His name snapped through the conference room like the crack of a whip, issuing from the head of the table, where his father, Parker Kane, presided. Judging by the edge of irritation creasing his stony face, Mason suspected an important question had been asked and was now awaiting his reply.

Which was unfortunate, as he had no idea what had been said.

He heard a *ping* and glanced at the screen of his open laptop to see the flashing bubble of an Outlook instant message.

CWestbrook: Neil wants to know why we exceeded the budget for the FitLife stick pack ad set.

A rush of gratitude warmed his chest as he glanced at Charlotte, who, per protocol, was staring directly at her own laptop, fingers flying deftly over the keyboard.

"Apologies." Mason summoned what he hoped was the proper level of self-effacing contrition. "I'm afraid I'm still waiting for some performance metrics back on that Instagram ad campaign your team recommended, but I'll be sure to pass it along as soon as I have that information."

From the other end of the table, his twin brother, Samuel—the CEO—made a sound that was neither a cough nor a snort but somehow managed to communicate his calling *bullshit* all the same.

It was unwelcome, if not entirely unjustified, because Mason—the Kane family's self-styled playboy, wastrel and all-around ne'er-do-well—had frequently used this tactic to buy time when asked a question he hadn't bothered preparing to answer. This chronic underachievement, an ongoing symptom of his abiding dislike for the corporate world in general, had reached a howling peak following a sequence of recent events.

The advent of Neil, his sister Marlowe's fiancé, being one of them.

With his dark hair, zealously manscaped eyebrows and aggressively tailored suits, Neil Campbell looked like the kind of almost-handsome douche yuppie who jerked it to *The Wolf of Wall Street*.

A relatively new addition to the executive team via an acquisition via Campbell Capital, Neil had immediately set about inserting his narrow blade of a nose so far up their father's ass, it was a wonder Parker could sit. What Mason's sister saw in him, other than their father's bland approval, beat the hell out of Mason.

Neil cleared his throat, deliberately leaning into Mason's eye line. "I was under the impression that data was published last Friday."

"Kind of you to bring that to my attention, Neil," Mason said in his World's Most Charming Bastard tone, with an accompanying grin, immeasurably glad Marlowe wasn't in the room to see right through him. "I'll be sure to review it at my earliest convenience."

Mason shifted his attention back to his laptop and tapped out a quick reply to Charlotte's message.

MKane: You saved my ass. I owe you.

On the other side of the table, Charlotte quickly silenced her laptop when it chirped. Now, her cheeks weren't just flushed, they were radioactive crimson.

He couldn't help but wonder if that hectic color would spill down her neck and breasts given the right provocation.

An ellipsis appeared in the space below his message, indicating she was in the process of composing a reply. To his amusement, Mason could hear by the rhythm of her fingers on the keys that she typed several lines before rapidly deleting them, settling in the end for:

CWestbrook: Not at all.

He would have given his antique Bulova watch to know what exactly she had been typing.

MKane: I mean it. What'll it be? Coffee? A Bentley?

A smile as brief and bright as a camera flash blazed across her lips, a welcome start to the quick round of electronic ping-pong that followed.

CWestbrook: It's totally fine, I promise.

MKane: You didn't answer my question.

CWestbrook: I'll get back to you on that.

He read the noncommittal reply, sensing the deliberate verbal smoke screen. No way was he letting her off the hook that easy.

Yes, he typed, every keystroke landing with the inevitability of a prophecy. You will.

Charlotte peered at him over the lid of her laptop.

Their eyes met and held.

He wished he could preserve her just as she was in that moment. Her velvety lips parted ever so slightly. Lashes lowered as she looked at him beneath the dark rims of her glasses. Her eyes sparkling with the mischief of their secret conversation.

"Did you get that, Miss Westbrook?"

The way Charlotte instinctively flinched at the sound of his father's voice made Mason suddenly, violently angry.

"I'm sorry," she said, casting an apologetic glance toward the head of the table. "Would you mind repeating that?"

Guilt pooled in his stomach like acid. Had he been paying closer attention, he could have come riding to her rescue as she had his.

His father sighed, managing to pack staggering amounts of frustration and disdain into that single sound. "We're moving the steering committee meeting to the third week of August."

"Yes, of course." Charlotte slid into the smooth, unfailingly polite and competent tone she used when answering his father's phone line.

"I trust you won't neglect to check the meeting link before sending the updated invitation this time," his father said, his voice barbed with rebuke.

Her shoulders rounded forward as if shrinking from the glowering, glacier-eyed, pewter-haired Kane patriarch. "Yes, sir," she said, her cheeks sporting an entirely different shade of blotchy red now. "I'll be sure to do so."

It had been a simple mistake. The kind of copy/paste error that literally every person seated around the table had committed at some point.

This didn't matter at all to his father, who had a particular way of memorizing missteps. And bringing them to your attention when they could cause maximum humiliation.

Mason knew this feeling intimately, though his father's disapproval had been aimed at his studious twin brother, Samuel, more often in their formative years. But ever since Mason had effectively placed his own neck on the chopping block to prevent his brother from being forced out of Kane Foods International following his open defiance of their father's cardinal no-company-romances rule, that dynamic had shifted drastically.

True, the fallout of Arlie and Samuel becoming an item had been very public and smeared with scandal, but the uproar had died quickly when the voracious public appetite for socially sullied billionaires found its next unfortunate target.

All that remained was his father's grudge at having his hand forced by his own son.

And Parker Kane's grudges were legendary.

Voices rose around him as the meeting began breaking into separate conversations, plans discussed for follow-up calls and breakout sessions.

Noting Charlotte's still-deflated posture, Mason found himself typing again, unsure of what, exactly, his intentions were.

MKane: Do you have a minute to chat after the meeting?

Her eyes flicked to her laptop. After a beat of hesitation, she replied.

CWestbrook: I'm afraid I have to cut out a little early today. Urgent?

He told himself it wasn't disappointment, this strange sinking feeling.

MKane: Not urgent. Another time?

CWestbrook: You bet.

People were pushing back from the table now, gathering their phones and long-since-depleted coffee cups.

Charlotte stood, hugging her laptop and notepad to her chest...much to Mason's regret. Still, this afforded him the opportunity to appraise the lower half of her standard uniform, consisting of a neat A-line skirt and strenuously practical heels.

The colors and prints of her button-up blouses varied, but never the rest of the outfit. Today, it was a slate-gray skirt, a light blue blouse with the slimmest of pinstripes, two-tone gray-and-black sling-backs.

Quickly gathering his own items, he swung around the edge of the table and followed Charlotte to the door, hurrying forward to open it for her in an effort so obvious he inwardly cringed.

"Thank you." She ducked her head, and he caught the fragrant mix of her clean, floral shampoo, something soft and citrusy beneath. Had he not covertly studied her at some length, he might have missed the subtle flick of her eyes as they moved over his torso.

Having inherited his father's lanky six-foot-three frame, Mason had done his level best to add layers of muscle through rigorous workouts with a personal trainer—aided vastly by his recent nocturnal activities.

"My pleasure," he said, hoping she didn't catch the subtle rasp in his voice.

He held back for a beat, wanting to let her get a few paces ahead of him.

In the time he'd begun casually observing her, he'd found that he loved watching her walk.

She moved like a dancer. Feet gliding forward, shapely calves flexing, hips swiveling sinuously side to side in an infinite loop through space.

Guilt stung him as he drank her in.

Not because he was mentally transgressing his father's cardinal rule.

Because he was transgressing his own.

Never press the advantage afforded to him by the executive status he had neither earned, nor wanted.

Despite his best efforts, Mason felt the building charge of arousal he'd prevented himself from slaking for months on end. A low, sparking electrical current. A coiled spring at the base of his spine.

Denial kept him hungry. Kept him hard.

He desperately needed to fuck or fight. Soon, he'd have the chance.

Because he, too, had somewhere to be tonight.

Somewhere he shouldn't.

Two

Yes. You will.

The words had been playing on repeat in Charlotte Westbrook's mind since she'd seen them flash on the screen of her laptop. There they had stayed on the commuter train from downtown Philadelphia to the parking lot in the suburb of Lansdale where she left her car five days a week.

The words were accompanied by a mental picture of Mason Kane's face.

Only the descriptions she frequently used in the novels she wrote at night and in stolen moments at work seemed to apply in describing him.

A chiseled jaw. A wickedly sensuous mouth. Perpetually wind-tossed dark hair, the ends kissed by the sun. Eyes of moss green with coronas of molten gold around the dark wells of his pupils. The kind of body she could easily imagine in the kilt of a highland laird, the tawny leather breeches of a Viking or pirate.

Imagine, she did.

Imagine, she had.

Frequently.

A fact that, to her complete and utter humiliation, Mason now seemed to know. In the two years she'd been working as his father's executive assistant, she had frequently enjoyed stolen glances at the younger Kane twin in a myriad of settings. In meetings. At corporate cocktail mixers. In hotel lobbies and bars and— occasionally—his office, which was her favorite of all. Something about the way he slouched at his desk was at once completely wrong for the polished setting and a living rebuke against anyone who would dare tell him so.

Apparently, her covert-observation privileges had been revoked.

Cringing as she got into her Honda Civic and started the engine, she relived his roguish smirk when he'd caught her furtive glances at the meeting today. Her stomach performed a delicate, top-of-the-roller-coaster flutter at the memory.

She had never been so grateful in all her life to have a reason to hightail it out of there directly after the meeting, even if it had cost her the icy disapproval of Parker Kane.

Charlotte pulled up to the curb in front of the duplex and unloaded her trunk. Her arms were full of grocery bags, and the summer heat clung to her hair as she unlocked the door. Kicking it closed behind her, she dropped her keys in the glass bowl on the entryway table and slung the bags on the kitchen counter before quickly returning to relock it.

"Surprise," said a voice right behind her.

Shrieking, she clutched at her chest as her arms flew up instinctively. Relief washed over her when her adrenaline-addled brain matched the voice with a face both familiar and welcome.

"Jesus, Jamie." She slugged her brother's wiry biceps. "You can't scare me like that."

"I'm sorry," he said, grinning at her as he massaged his arm. "I just wanted to surprise you."

"Well, mission accomplished." Heart still pounding, she wrapped him in a fierce hug, grateful for the instant comfort of his presence.

Even if his ever-stylish wardrobe always made her feel like a boring, corporate schlub.

Today he wore a slim-fit, short-sleeved button-up shirt in an eye-frying pattern only he could pull off, stylishly tattered skinny jeans and Gucci slides. How he always seemed to be able to afford designer labels on a moderately successful ceramicist's salary never ceased to amaze her.

On a gusty exhale, she padded into the kitchen to put the groceries away. "You nearly gave me a heart attack."

"That would be far less likely if you listened to me about your appalling exercise habits." Jamie plopped down on a stool at the breakfast bar facing into the small galley kitchen, exactly as he had when they were kids. Knobby elbows on the bar, puckish chin propped on the heels of his hands, tufted blond hair almost platinum under the small fluorescent tube light over the sink.

"I work fifty hours a week, have an hour-long com-

mute on either side, take care of Mom in the evenings
and am also trying to write books." She dug into the
nearest bag, pulled out a carton of eggs and milk and
slid them into the fridge. "Forgive me for not finding
time to establish a fitness regimen as well."

"How's that going, by the way?" He took a tangerine from the bowl of fruit on the counter and dug his
thumb into the center to loosen the peel.

"Which part?" she snorted, stacking cans of soup in
the small closet pantry.

"The book." He popped a wedge into his mouth.

The book that was absolutely, positively *not* about
Mason Kane.

Yes, the hero was a ridiculously attractive billionaire who might bear the *slightest* resemblance to him
physically, but that's where the similarities ceased. *Her*
billionaire was dark, and brooding, and hiding a terrible secret.

She shrugged. "It's basically a heap of flaming gar-
bage that will probably never see the light of day, but
I'm delusional enough to keep going, for some reason."

"You say that about every book, Charlie," he said,
chewing. "What are you, about one-third of the way
through?"

"Not that I'm hesitant to unpack my dysfunctional
creativity with you, but what are you even doing here,
anyway?" she asked, annoyed that he knew precisely
how to call her on her bullshit. "I can't believe you just
came all the way from Boston on a whim."

Jamie set the tangerine aside, pushing the bits of peel
around with his index finger. "David and I broke up."

"Again?" Charlotte had been on the receiving end of

so many late-night calls and desperate texts throughout the six months of the David-and-Jamie saga that she could scarcely keep up.

"It's different this time," Jamie said.

"Different how?"

"Well, you remember how he usually leaves something of his so he has an excuse to come back, and when he does I somehow forget how much it hurts when he's self-centered and unavailable and remember how hot he is when he's all heartbroken and broody?" he asked.

"How could I forget?" She folded the empty paper bags and opened the cupboard under the sink to put them in the designated recycling bag.

"He didn't leave anything this time." The genuine sadness in her brother's normally effusive voice tugged at her heart.

"Wow," she said. "I'm really sorry, Jamie."

Jamie nodded, his hazel eyes luminescent with unshed tears. He waved the emotion away, quickly rising from the stool.

"So, anyway," he said, gathering the tangerine shrapnel into his palm and carrying it to the trash. "I thought I could come to Philly for a while, take some time to process, find another beautiful but narcissistic and emotionally withholding out-of-work musician to rebound with. And hang out with you and Mom, of course."

Charlotte snapped at his butt with a rolled-up dishtowel.

Jamie caught the end of it and yanked it from her grasp. "Speaking of, where is Mom?"

"She's out with Gail. They go to the park on Thursday afternoons." Sweet, patient, and unfailingly kind, her mother's caregiver, like the weekly routine she had established, had become an integral part of Charlotte's existence.

An uncharacteristically serious expression softened Jamie's face. "*How* is she?"

Charlotte sighed, her hands resting on the faux-granite counter. There was no tidy answer to this question.

Diagnosed with Alzheimer's three years prior, their mother had initially only required help for a few hours a day. Someone to make sure she'd eaten, taken her meds, opened her mail. But when the end of year two rolled around, she'd taken a hairpin turn into unreality.

Wandering the streets of Lansdale, losing faces, forgetting names.

Which was when Charlotte had moved back into her childhood home with her.

"She's…struggling," she said.

Jamie drew in a solemn breath. "You know you're not going to be able to keep doing this forever."

"I know." She draped the towel over the sink. "I just want her to stay in her home as long as possible."

Even as she said it, she knew this wasn't entirely true. What Charlotte wanted, if she were being brutally honest with herself, was for the home and its memories to remain in her mother. The mock cherry tree in the backyard she had planted back when she still had hobbies, and gardening was one of them. The antique desk with the old typewriter where Charlotte had laboriously typed her first story about Burt the cow dog, the clicking of those keys scratching a previously unacknowledged itch deep inside her brain.

Finding reliable caregivers to look after her mother

for the ten hours a day Charlotte belonged to Parker Kane had been difficult and expensive, despite the long-term-care insurance. But every now and then, when they sat together bathed in the silvery glow of the TV, watching the black-and-white classics their mother loved so well, she would surprise Charlotte by telling her where she had first seen the movie, or whom she'd been with.

"Well," Jamie said, opening the refrigerator door and pulling out a bag of baby carrots. "Tonight, you're off duty. I'm going to cook us something I'll have to apologize to my trainer for, and then after Mom's in bed, we'll watch Brit coms in our jammies just like old times."

"Actually," she said, already preparing herself for his reaction, "I have plans."

"Plans?" He arched an eyebrow. "What kind of plans?"

"A date." Though, technically speaking, *date* wasn't exactly accurate. *A painstakingly arranged rendezvous in the name of book research after months of covert wrangling* would be closer to the truth.

"You dirty whore." Jamie lobbed a baby carrot at her. "You've been holding out on me! Who is he? Tell me everything."

"His name is Bentley Drake. He's a lawyer. I met him at Starbucks." *After cyberstalking him when I learned he may be connected with an underground executive box- ing ring that I've been trying to break into for months* was the part she chose not to share with her brother.

"Bentley Drake," he repeated, trying it on. "That name has some serious big-dick energy."

"I wouldn't know," Charlotte said. What she did

know was that, on the outside, Bentley Drake resembled a chiseled, icy-eyed, shadow-jawed maybe-mafioso. Complete with a fine silver scar slicing through the arc of one dark eyebrow.

She really wished that did something for her.

Wished that literally *anyone* other than the smirking, bed-hopping, totally-off-limits Mason Kane could manage to turn her engine over.

"So is this a first date?" her brother asked.

"Are you suggesting that if it wasn't, I would have slept with him already?" Folding her arms across her chest, Charlotte pinned him with a pointed look.

"No judgment." He lifted his hands in mock surrender. "I'm just really glad to see you getting out there again after Trent."

Hearing her ex's name spoken aloud landed like a punch to her solar plexus. Trent Bateman had been Charlotte's only long-term relationship. Her boyfriend for the last half of college and both years of grad school, their union had been the equivalent of a three-car pileup followed by a head-on collision. The kind where one of the vehicles catches fire and burns to a blackened shell.

That vehicle being her.

Discovering that Trent had cheated on her had been one thing. But that he'd cheated on her multiple times because she'd been so focused on school that he'd felt neglected and lonely?

A masterpiece of emotional manipulation.

The aftermath had left her a needy, weepy, self-conscious wreck who had alienated almost every human save her brother, and dating hadn't been a priority.

In two years since, her life had been work, and words, and little else.

"To answer your question, it's not even really a date. It's research." She began plucking out the small army of bobby pins that held her smooth ballet bun in place, relishing the feeling of the tension easing from her scalp.

"Does *he* know he's research?" Grimacing, Jamie set the carrots aside and plucked a grapefruit shandy from the fridge door, twisting the cap off with a quick jerk.

"He knows that he wanted to spend an evening with me, and that is precisely what he'll be doing." Dropping the last of the pins on the counter, she shook out her hair, relishing soft feel of it against the backs of her arms as the ends tickled her elbows.

Jamie coughed out a mouthful of foam, wiping it with the back of his hand. "Holy shit, your hair's gotten long."

"Which is exactly why I don't have time to talk." Brushing past him, she made her way down the hall toward the bathroom, unbuttoning her blouse on the way. "It takes forever to curl."

Twenty minutes later, makeup refreshed, hair falling in soft, vine-like tangles down her back, Charlotte asked Jamie to help zip her into her skintight, cleavage-bearing black cocktail dress.

"And where is this nondate taking place?" he asked.

"It's a secret," she said, meeting his eye in the full-length mirror and giving him a mysterious smile. She crouched down, examining her orderly racks of shoes. Remembering that Bentley Drake cleared six feet, she selected a pair of sleek black stilettos, the peep-toe revealing the barest glimpse of nails polished a ludicrous fire-engine red.

Jamie took a swig of his shandy and let fly a wet whistle. "Well, I hope poor Bentley doesn't fall ass-over-latte in love the second he sees you. That would certainly be a damper in the research department."

Not necessarily, Charlotte thought, reaching down to shimmy the snug fabric of her dress down her freckle-flecked thighs.

Because Bentley Drake wasn't the target of her research.

He was only her entry ticket to The League.

The League.

An underground, rich boys–only mixed martial arts ring.

She'd first heard whispers of it at Philadelphia's Engine 32 fire department, where she'd hung around when working on a different novel. Sacrificing sleep between the hours of 10:00 p.m. and 5:00 a.m. to observe honest-to-God firemen in their natural habitat. To know the reality of their life.

There, during the gray, naked hours before early dawn, she overheard them. Pretending to sleep in a threadbare armchair, she'd concentrated on mimicking a deep, regular breathing pattern while they discussed "bets" and "horses" in a way that gave her to know they weren't discussing racing at all but the elusive and exclusive billionaires' fight club.

Slowly, and with the precision of a bomb technician, she'd begun tugging threads, until they led her to Bentley Drake. Who, with a bravado that made her writer's antennae twitch, informed her that he *might* be able to get her access. *If* the club owners believed she was someone he knew "very well."

A requirement that, after the twelve hours she'd once spent staked out in the car of a private detective while working on a mystery novel, seemed infinitely doable.

"Is he coming to pick you up?" Jamie sank down on the edge of her bed, the brown bottle sweating in his hand.

"I'm meeting him downtown." Checking herself one last time, she faced her brother. "Gail and Mom should be home by seven. Whatever you do, whatever Mom says, don't correct her. She gets very agitated."

Jamie held up two fingers. "Scout's honor."

"Like you were ever a Boy Scout," she snorted, clicking her way back toward the living room to gather her purse and keys. "There's my ride."

Glancing down at the transportation app on her phone, she dropped it into a bag of the size Bentley told her was allowed by The League's incredibly stringent security protocol.

"Wait one sec." Setting his shandy down on the coffee table, Jamie dug in the clay-flecked backpack slung at the base of the oversize living room couch before approaching her with a slim black cylinder clutched in his fist. "Take this."

"Pepper spray?" she asked, half laughing as she flipped up the safety nozzle.

"Be careful." Jamie plucked it from her grip and slid it into her evening bag.

Leaning forward, she planted a quick peck on his cheek. "I always am," she lied.

Bentley Drake was early.

He leaned against an unassuming brick building, the

bottom of one expensive loafer against the granite, the other anchored against the sidewalk like a kickstand. The crisp white shirt showed off a torso clearly honed by years in the gym. His powerful legs were on full display in expertly tailored charcoal-gray slacks, about two inches of his tanning bed–bronzed ankle visible below the creased cuff of his trouser. His coal-black hair was a hue suspiciously consistent, his goatee just a shade too neat.

She fought a yawn.

Goddamn you, Mason Kane.

"You made it." It was the voice he used in his commercials. Confident. Resonant. Assuring you that, if you were in an automobile accident, you, too, could recover as much as two hundred thousand dollars in damages. He held his hand out to her.

She took it, suppressing a shiver when their palms glided over one another like he'd lotioned mere moments before her arrival.

"I said I would," she said.

Not missing a beat, Bentley turned, tucking her arm under his and placing her hand on his forearm.

A mix of expensive cologne and eager male expectation drifted over to her on the balmy night air. "There are a few things I need to tell you about The League before we arrive."

Under the anemic glow of streetlamps, she allowed herself to be escorted, waiting for his inevitable recitation of information she'd already been able to piece together on her own.

"I'm all ears." Hating herself a little, Charlotte tossed her head in the way that sent her hair swinging like a curtain of silk.

"We don't use names," Bentley said as they approached what looked to be an abandoned warehouse. "All fighters choose a pseudonym."

"What's yours?" she asked, allowing herself to be guided down a set of stairs.

"Don John." By the meaningful look he cut her way, Charlotte understood the Shakespearean origins were meant to impress her.

"I had no idea you were so literary," she said.

He raked her with a suggestive stare. "There's a lot you don't know about me."

She would have preferred to keep it that way, but she was eager to nudge this part of the evening along. "You mentioned before that bets are placed on each of the matches?"

"That's right," he said. "You're given a card upon entry. You pick your 'horse' and fill in how much you're willing to wager. Then, you watch."

A wave of relief washed over her. This, she could do.

"Of course, there's a minimum," he added. "But The League's spectators don't generally find this to be a problem."

"How much?" she asked, a hot wire tightening around her stomach. This particular bit of information was news to her.

Bentley laughed. It was the arrogant, unrestricted guffaw of a man for whom such questions represented the height of amusement.

"Ten thousand per fight, per attendee."

Charlotte froze in her tracks. She felt the swell of panic that only a child who has watched their parent have to choose items to put back at the grocery store checkout lane knows. "Oh. I didn't know—"

"Shh." Bentley pressed a fingertip to her lips. "Do you honestly think I would have invited you if I weren't willing to foot the bill?"

"Why?" Charlotte asked, trying not to taste the perfumey liniment on his skin.

"Because," he replied, dragging his finger down her chin. "I find you intriguing."

"That's very—" Her throat worked over a swallow beneath his smooth fingers traveling from her jaw to her clavicle. "Kind of you."

"Kind? No." His hand was heavy on her shoulder. "But I know a favorable investment when I see one."

For the book, she reminded herself. *This is all for your book.*

She lowered her eyelids, deepened her voice, pretending the kind of boldness she invented for a woman she wasn't. "Thank you, Bentley."

"You can thank me later." The words dripped with suggestion as he backed away from her, wrapping a possessive arm around her back, fingertips octopussuctioned onto her hip.

At the end of a low-ceilinged hallway plastered with tattered posters, they reached a set of wooden double doors.

Bentley rapped on the one with a metal slot at eye level and held up a golden key.

The doors slid open.

She felt a whoosh of body heat and noise roll over her, the dull hum of a hundred conversations backed by ambient music designed to be ignored.

At a kiosk not unlike a coat check, a slim pen and stiff, creamy card were pressed into her hand before Bentley steered her to the bar. It was a long, glossy, wooden affair that put her in mind of libraries and speakeasies and the places men drank expensively with their mistresses.

"What can I get you?" The sleek blonde bartender's eyes flicked over Bentley as she splayed slim fingers over the bar top. Like it was an extension of his body she was touching.

"I'll have a double bourbon," he said, clearly not giving the bartender the kind of attention she was used to receiving from him, "neat."

"A single bourbon for me," she said. "But with a rock."

Judging by the ludicrously white smile he beamed down at Charlotte, she might have just informed him he'd won the lottery.

With a huff of exasperation, the bartender bustled off to get their drinks.

When she was gone, Bentley pressed his card to the glossy bar top. "So," he asked magnanimously. "Who are we betting on?"

Charlotte squinted at the card, irritation hot at the back of her neck before she realized there was zero chance of her reading it without her glasses. Stabbing an irritated hand into her tiny bag, she slid her emergency reading glasses onto her face. Slowly, the names swam into focus.

She ran a nail down the card, stopping when she reached Remus Pax.

A little shiver worked its way down her back for no reason she could explain.

"This one," she said.

A scowl creased Bentley's artificially tanned cheeks. There and gone as quickly as a lightning strike.

"The lady decides." Using the pen provided, he made a tick mark next to Remus Pax on both of their cards. "How much are we wagering?"

The bartender returned with their drinks, slopping some of Charlotte's over the rim and onto her card.

"Oh, shoot," she said, mopping the bar in mock regret. "I am *so* sorry."

Charlotte felt a spurt of pity for this woman whose chief resolution of petty jealousy was passive-aggressive drink service. Frankly, she knew the feeling.

"No apologies necessary," she said, squeezing Bentley's biceps and instantly regretting it as his fingers tightened over her hip.

Charlotte lifted the glass of amber liquid, relishing the ice bobbing against her lips. "It's your call," she said, trying to flick her eyes away demurely as she backed out of his grip.

"Fifty thousand?"

In the versions of this scene she'd rehearsed in her mind, she had not executed a perfect spit take, atomizing expensive bourbon in a brief, tawny cloud. She found herself in imminent danger of doing so.

"I can do that, you know." Pulling her body closer to his, he brushed the curtain of her hair over her shoulder. "I could lose a million and still be okay."

He said this as if it would impress rather than sicken her.

"You would wager that much on a *horse* you don't even like?" she asked.

"Did I say I didn't like him?" Bentley lifted his drink to his lips, sipping silently.

She smiled at him despite herself. "You didn't have to."

He rewarded her with an indulgent grin. "Whether I like him or not doesn't matter. It's whether he wins."

"And does he?" she asked.

"Only other undefeated fighter in The League," Bentley said. "Other than yours truly."

"Even so," she said. "There's no reason to wager so much of your hard-earned money on my account."

"But there is." He wound a lock of her hair around his finger, the buffed nail at its tip faintly gleaming. "To show you what I have to give."

A cold dread hardened in her stomach. Her options were few.

Leave now. Abandon all efforts to infiltrate the club she had chipped away at for the better part of a year. Take her pride and her research and hit the road.

Or stay. Stay, and try.

She tried.

The night crept along at a maddening pace. Labored conversation, men laughing indulgently during the lesser skirmishes, women wearing small, tight, candy-colored dresses on their arms. A roped-off platform at the center of the club featured an ever-shifting cast of characters, each as forgettable as the ones before.

Until the rich tones of an announcer's voice cut through the cigar smoke, announcing the main event.

Remus Pax vs. Man o' War.

Two double bourbons in, Bentley seemed distinctly annoyed. At the notes Charlotte had insisted on tapping into her phone. At her unfinished first drink sweating on the table between them.

She wasn't keeping up her end of the "date."

In a reluctant gesture of deference to her host, she put her phone away, sipping at the watery bourbon.

"There's our horse." Bentley breathed high-proof fumes into her ear.

Glancing in the direction of Bentley's focus, she blinked, and blinked again, somehow believing that if she did so, the specter dancing before her eyes would change.

It didn't.

Long-legged and deep-chested, Remus Pax had a photo-realistic tattoo of a wolf eating up the broad terrain of his left pectoral muscle, swirls like gusts of the night wind and the moon beyond spiraling down to the crook of his left elbow. Next to it, the washboard of his abdominal muscles disappeared into his black athletic shorts in a dangerous V.

Remus Pax was Mason Kane.

Mason Kane as she had never before seen him. All traces of levity and mischief were absent from his features. His eyes fastened onto his opponent as if they were the only two humans who existed in the entire cosmos.

That intense stare lasering into the thing he wanted to destroy.

It was there. All there.

The broad, winged back she had imagined pressing her hand to beneath the expensive fabric of his shirt. The long, smooth neck that had so often teased her into wondering what his skin would taste like just beneath his starched collar. Lips she had seen smirk and tease and tempt, puffed out by a black protective mouth guard.

"He's tougher than he looks," Bentley informed her, misdiagnosing her shock as doubt. "He founded The League."

Then there was a bell.

How intoxicating to watch him move. Mason ducked and feinted with an almost fox-like smoothness, a ruthless but fleet-footed grace. In a series of moves almost too quick for her to follow, he drove his left fist then his right into Man o' War's rib cage, following it with a quick upward jab that snapped the other man's dark-haired head abruptly backward.

His opponent lurched and staggered, and then, in a stroke of unaccountable luck, clipped Mason's jaw, sending a bright red spray of blood from the corner of his mouth.

Charlotte cried out, slapping a hand to her lips, but not before that one disastrous syllable escaped her. "Mas—"

It was too late.

His eyes found hers milliseconds before a fist crashed into his temple.

The green-gold eyes she'd deliberately dodged a thousand times rolled up toward his skull, the whites overtaking all.

Limbs folding, his body crumpled into an unceremonious heap on the crimson-flecked canvas.

Bentley snarled beside her even as Man o' War's bloody fist was hoisted to the sky.

"I'm so sorry," Charlotte said, aware that it wasn't the loss of Bentley Drake's bet she was apologizing for.

She had cost Mason his perfect record.

A man with salt-and-pepper hair and a determined expression had joined Mason in the ring, mopping his face with a wet towel and coaxing him into a seated position.

And damned if, the second he regained consciousness, Mason wasn't searching the crowd in her general direction, even as he was escorted out of the ring and down a side hallway at the back of the buzzing crowd.

Her head felt light and her stomach heavy as she turned to Bentley. "I have to go," she said.

"Oh, no, you don't." The veneer of practiced smoothness faltered, and beneath it, she caught a glimpse of something angry, dark and expectant.

Manage this. Now.

"I do," she said, caressing his forearm. "I don't feel very well. But I promise to feel so much better next time I see you."

The crease in his tanned brow smoothed even as he squeezed her hip with painful force. "I'm sure you will."

Charlotte forced herself to smile at him before making a beeline for the door.

And, just when she'd nearly reached it, she stole a look back at Bentley, who had once again captured the attention of their buxom bartender.

Stepping out of her heels, Charlotte wove her way into the crush of bodies until she reached the corridor she'd seen Mason half carried down.

With a quick glance in either direction, she slipped into the oddly silent hallway, her ear pressed to an unmarked door until she heard his voice.

She didn't bother to knock.

What they had to discuss was important enough to trump such trivial social constructs. Anyway, there was no guarantee she would have been granted entry had she announced herself.

She pressed her palm against the door, satisfied when it swung smoothly inward.

Mason sat on a wooden bench, a bucket of ice before him and the silver-haired man beside him, the white towel pressed to his eyebrow sprouting a growing spot of poppy red.

He sat bolt upright when he spotted her, his spine stiffening.

His manager—or so she had come to think of him—informed her that she couldn't be in here. That she needed to leave immediately.

"She can stay." Mason grinned at her with split lips slightly swelling on one side. Then, to her complete horror, he patted the wooden bench beside him.

Suddenly, she wished she'd listened to his manager.

Carrying her heels in one hand, she padded across the concrete floor and seated herself a reassuring two feet away. To be so close to Mason's naked skin felt shockingly intimate.

"Well, Charlotte Westbrook." Dropping the bloodied towel into the ice bucket, Mason turned his sweat-kissed face to her. "You just cost me two hundred thousand dollars."

Three

Mason had been hit plenty of times since joining The League six months ago.

Jabs. Crosses. Hooks. Uppercuts.

Not a single punch could compare to the shock of catching Charlotte's eye in the middle of the crowd.

A knockout.

He used to think of this as a shallow, trite way to describe a beautiful woman. Now he understood. A beauty so unexpected, so blinding, so universe-altering that it relieves you of your consciousness.

And on the arm of Bentley *fucking* Drake. His rival in The League.

"I'm really sorry." She tugged at the hem of a dress shorter than anything he'd ever seen her wear, acres of long, pale, lightly freckled legs tucked primly beneath the bench.

"You should be," he scolded playfully. "You cost me my perfect record."

Reaching up, she pushed a russet lock over her shoulder where it fell all the way to her elbow. The need to plunge his fingers into that silky, sweet-scented mass and follow it from scalp to tips gnawed at him.

From the corner, his booker cleared his throat. "You want a ride to urgent care?"

"I'm okay, Ralph," Mason said dismissively.

"You could have a concussion." Charlotte squinted at him as if she might be able to confirm the diagnosis visually. "Do you feel nausea? Dizziness? Confusion?"

Truly, he felt all these, but not for the reasons she thought. "Confused about what the hell you're doing here," he said.

"I could say the same." She treated him to a saucy sideways glance that only tossed gasoline on the glowing coals of his interest. "What about that cut above your eyebrow?"

Without so much as asking permission, she retrieved the wet, cold towel from the bucket and scooted close enough to dab gently at his face. Heat radiated from her creamy cleavage as she leaned into him, and he smelled the subtle, smoky sweetness of bourbon on her breath.

His mouth flooded with saliva at the prospect of tasting it on her tongue.

"You lucked out," she said, setting the rag aside. "It's not deep enough to need stitches. Do you have a first aid kit?" She glanced over her shoulder at Ralph.

Ralph started as if he, too, had been caught in the spell of her unexpected presence. "I really think I should be the one to—"

"Just give it to her," Mason ordered. In no small part because the idea of the fragrant creature before him being replaced by leather-skinned, perpetually onion-scented Ralph filled him with instant outrage.

Obediently, Ralph set down the plastic case next to her, grumbling under his breath as he shoved his way out into the hall.

Charlotte riffled through the first aid supplies with expert efficiency. "Can you turn toward me?" she asked, reaching into her small, beaded evening bag to retrieve a smaller version of the sleek black frames she wore at work and sliding them on her face.

The contrast between those studious glasses and her seductress dress threatened to unman him on the spot.

Mason did as he was bidden, lifting a leg to straddle the bench. She remained sidesaddle, knees and ankles pressed together. Because, dear God, had she mimicked his pose, he'd be able to see all the way to her—

Don't. Fucking. Go. There.

He stepped hard on the thought. Particularly because he'd already removed his protective cup and the light, breathable shorts he wore for fighting would conceal exactly nothing should he develop a problem.

"So are you a field nurse when you're not putting up with my father?" he asked, relishing the way her cheeks colored his favorite shade of lightly spanked pink.

"I was a nursing student, once upon a time." She tore the top off a sanitizing wipe, nimble fingers setting out packets of antibiotic ointment, surgical tape strips and gauze. "Before I switched to English lit. This is going to sting a little."

He hissed as the sharp tang of alcohol invaded his nostrils and he felt the bright, hot burn above his eyebrow.

"Sorry about that." The iridescent glob of the ointment she gently spread across the offended tissue of his wound provided immediate relief.

"What made you choose English lit?" he asked, desperate to keep the conversation as mundane as possible.

"A desire to significantly limit my career options." She flicked a shy smirk at him. "Also, I absolutely loved it."

"I know how that goes." But he didn't, really. He'd completed exactly one semester as a fine arts student before being called into his father's study to be gently bullied into changing his major to the more practical marketing program.

Mason snapped back to the present. Having Charlotte so close, her hands so near his face, her mouth mere inches from him, was driving him mad.

It had been so long.

He'd kept up appearances, of course, squiring socialites and lady executives to bars, clubs, balls and concerts. His reputation demanded it. And he got them off. In coat checks. The backs of limousines. In elevators and velvet-roped VIP rooms. With his hands, his mouth. Which had the ironic effect of redoubling their tenacity.

Madison Bradford in particular. Former model and current dilettante. Once occupying the top rung of his call-in-case-of-emergency list, she'd grown more and more impatient with the change of their former arrangement. His excuses had become more vague as her calls and texts grew more frequent. And graphic.

At times, remembering some of their more adventurous encounters, he'd been tempted to give in just once.

But with Madison, it never was just once.

Now it had been months since he'd last been with a woman.

Months on end of going home hard. Hungry. All that boiling, ravenous need. He'd harvested it all. Pushed it down, down to the base of his stomach where, once he got in the ring, it detonated in a thrillingly vicious charge. Burning off a measure of the poison he couldn't seem to drain by another means.

"Is it?"

By the way she said it, Mason could tell she was repeating the question.

"What's that?" he asked.

"You really do struggle to pay attention." Her lush lips twisted in a smirk, a dimple flashing briefly at the corner of her mouth. "Is it okay if I rest my elbow on your shoulder so I can hold your eyebrow taut? It's a lot easier to put the tape on that way."

"You can rest your elbow wherever you please."

He winced inwardly, hating how weak this invitation had sounded.

God, Mason.

Don't be that guy.

Not now. Not with her.

This is your father's executive assistant, he reminded himself. *The woman upon whom the formidable Parker Kane relied to govern every minute of his work day and manage the minutia of his life beyond it.*

Possibly the single worst choice of a drought breaker in the entire city. Perhaps the entire planet. The human equivalent of a glowing red Danger! sign. Trouble with a capital T.

Only...

The flush had spread from Charlotte's cheeks down the creamy column of her neck. She leaned forward, her breasts so close to his face that he could see the subtle outline of her nipples, hard against the fabric of her dress.

Christ, he was in trouble.

He quickly slung his forearm over his lap and recalled every boner-killing image in his recently assembled catalog. It was the mental equivalent of a cold shower. But nothing succeeded in banishing the feeling of her cool, soft fingertips gently brushing his fevered brow.

The gentleness, the tenderness of that touch woke an ache he hadn't known he'd been ignoring.

"There," she said, casually brushing a lock of sweaty hair from his forehead. "Good as new."

At that moment, he would have given his entire trust fund to thumb down the neckline of her dress and suck her sweet, hard—

She snapped her fingers at him. A crease appeared at the center of her delicate eyebrows, the corners of her lips tugged downward, brown eyes wide with concern. "I really think we should take you to the ER. You keep zoning out."

"Really," he insisted. "I'm okay. I'll just get changed and take myself straight home."

"You are in absolutely no shape to drive yourself anywhere." Charlotte quickly gathered up the discarded bandage wrappers and dropped them in the small waste-basket by the door.

He couldn't help but notice how differently she moved when not constrained by her standard uniform. A more sensual version of her elegant, gliding gait.

"Is that an offer?" he shot back. "Or is Bentley waiting for you?"

Picturing the man proved to be the remedy Mason needed. Money-flashing, conquest-touting Bentley Drake of the boys' club, known for backslapping and his devotion to tanning beds.

Now the rosy glow spread to Charlotte's chest, spilling over the elegant ledges of her collarbones.

"I'm not— We're not. It wasn't a date. Not a real one."

"You don't owe me any explanations," Mason said, swinging his leg back over the bench. "Your time is your own. I would warn you that Bentley has somewhat of a…reputation where women are concerned."

"And you'd know nothing about that."

Mason wasn't sure who was more shocked by her retort.

Him, or Charlotte.

"I'm so sorry." She pressed a hand to her lips. "I didn't mean—"

"It's true." Reaching into his duffel bag, Mason grabbed a shirt and shrugged it over his head. "Although I must I admit I'm not familiar with what a *not real* date entails."

"Research." Charlotte put her heels on the floor before her and slid her bare feet into them, red-lacquered toes first.

"What kind of research?" he asked, unwinding his

hand wraps and dropping them into his bag without rolling them. He jammed his feet straight into the sneakers he kept in his gym bag, not wanting to bother with socks.

"Book research."

Arlie had informed him at a customer conference a few months back that Charlotte secretly wrote romance novels, books that tended toward the steamy.

This information hadn't helped keep his libido in check when paired with her frequent, furtive glances at him.

"About Bentley?" Mason teased.

"About The League." The strange, poignant ache deepened as Charlotte busied herself hanging up his discarded dress shirt and slacks, looping his tie over the hanger. "I overheard some firefighters talking about it and have been trying to work my way in here ever since."

A distinct filament of unease glowed in Mason's mind. "Firefighters?"

She arched a brow at him. "Also research."

"Huh," he said. "And what about The League might be of interest, researchwise, for your current project?"

"I'm...uh, not far enough along to talk about it, really."

Mason stood and was relieved when the room didn't spin and the floor remained firmly planted under his feet. "Oh, come on. I won't tell a soul." He mimed zipping his lips and drew a cross over his T-shirt in the approximate area of his heart.

"It's about a billionaire who's leading a double life, and he meets and falls in love with a woman who could potentially ruin everything by exposing his deep, dark secret."

"I see." Mason crossed the room and took the hanger from her. "And this character of yours. He wouldn't happen to be an executive of some kind?"

"He might," she admitted, shifting on her heels.

"If only you knew someone who even vaguely fit that description." He tapped his chin—carefully—with his index and middle fingers.

"Technically, that description could fit a lot of people." She glanced coolly around the room, all business. "Are your keys in the duffel bag?"

"Front pocket."

She brushed past him and hefted the bag to the bench, a fresh punch of lust hitting him low in the gut as she bent ever so slightly to dig through the pocket. Her slim hand emerged with her index finger hooked into the ring.

"Ready?" She started to lift the duffel bag, but he rushed over and grabbed it, his hand partially covering hers, awareness tingling in that small area of contact.

"No way are you carrying this for me," he said. "Concussion or no."

"If you insist." Releasing the handle, she slipped her hand free.

"To your left." He held the door open so she could exit, following her down a hallway leading away from the crowd to an elevator with direct access to a level of the parking garage concealed from the general public.

The gleaming steel doors opened, and they were together in the small, polished box. Mason's finger hovered over the button labeled "7G" but stopped short of pressing it.

Charlotte's eyebrows lifted in a curious expression.

"Can I ask you a question?" Mason said.

"You already have." Again, that quick flick of her eyes on his before they darted to the gleaming brass handrail. "Several, in fact."

"Today in the boardroom. Why did you message me the question that I missed?"

She shrugged. "You seemed distracted."

"I was." Two steps and he was across the elevator. Close enough to see the bright rings from the overhead lights reflected around the centers of her brown irises. "Do you know why?"

"Because…" She wet her lower lip with the pointed pink tip of her tongue. "You caught me looking at you."

"Why?" Mason put a hand under her jaw, tilting it upward. "Why are you *always* looking at me?"

Charlotte's eyes hid beneath the dark fan of lashes trimming her half-lowered lids.

"Because I like it," she breathed.

Those four words slid right through his stomach and rooted themselves at the base of his cock. He should stop now. Back away. Let this die. Make himself forget.

Because what good would it do him to remember when every conceivable obstacle existed between them? When his mind bellowed how completely, disastrously wrong this would be?

For her. For him. For everyone.

Yes. He *needed* to forget.

But he didn't want to.

Mason brushed his thumb over her cheekbone. "If you like it, why won't you look at me now?"

Her breath came in erratic puffs, her chest rising and falling haphazardly, her knuckles white as she clutched his keys. "I'm afraid."

"Of what?"

He hovered there, their breath mingling, mouths mere inches apart, when the elevator doors opened, and Man o' War entered, trailing a laugh and the pungent scent of weed.

"Well, if it isn't the man who made me two hundred K richer," he said, punching the 7G button. "Rotten luck, bro."

Mason's teeth ground together so hard that hot, white pain shot up through his jaw. "Wasn't my night."

"Seems like it will be later, though." Man o' War slid an oily glance over Charlotte. "I saw you with Don John earlier. If you're making your way down the roster—"

A red wall of rage rose around Mason, blocking out everything but the face he wanted to smash, a high-pitched buzzing filling his ears. He found himself with a handful of T-shirt, shoving Man o' War back against the elevator wall, pinning him with a forearm across the throat.

"You will shut your mouth or I will knock your teeth down your goddamn throat," he growled.

"You're not in the ring anymore, pretty boy." Man o' War's dark eyes narrowed, his thin lips twisted in a sneer. "No referee to save your ass this time."

"It's not *my* ass that needs saving." Mason leaned in, a savage bolt of satisfaction striking his brain at the rattling cough beneath his arm. "Apologize."

"Mason," Charlotte protested. "Please—"

"Apologize!"

"Sorry," Man o' War choked. "Get off me, man."

Mason released him just as the doors opened.

The other man stayed just a beat too long. An ugly smile carved a cavern in his pockmarked face. "See you around."

Charlotte exhaled audibly once he was gone, her face pallid and eyes wider than he'd ever seen them.

Mason put out his free arm to keep the elevator doors from closing. "I'm sorry if I scared you."

"You didn't." She walked past him into the parking garage, her heels echoing in the quiet concrete chamber as she glanced back over her shoulder. "I kind of liked that, too."

For that bare second, all her shyness seemed to be gone, and Mason caught a glimpse of a different side of her.

A fox.

Another outdated term often used for women men wanted to hunt and chase.

That was just what she reminded him of. A sleek, cunning creature with a golden-eyed gaze. Shy, sly and elusive.

Right up until she did the hunting.

Charlotte lifted his keys and pressed the unlock button until there was a chirp, which she followed to his car. Once there, she was all business, popping the trunk so he could deposit his duffel bag, hanging his clothes on the hook in the back seat.

She opened the driver's door before he had a chance, smoothly sliding into the seat. The Aston purred to life as Mason closed his door and buckled himself in with a sense of unreality. He had never been in the passenger's seat of his own car.

Charlotte could have been an actress in a driver's ed video, executing all the safety measures with efficient precision. Adjusting the driver's seat, checking the mirrors, familiarizing herself with the controls before turning to him.

The way her slim fingers closed around the steering wheel's buttery black leather woke a sympathetic ache in Mason's groin.

"Okay, Mason Kane," she said, her voice tinged with a playful lilt. "Where am I going?"

He looked at her, dizzy with her scent in the close air of Aston's interior. "To my bed."

Four

To my bed.

The words thickened the air between them, shocking Charlotte into silence.

Silence that spoke volumes more than any outraged objection on her part.

He knew.

There could be no doubt of it now. Not that there had been much to begin with. Her fingertips still burned from having touched his smooth, damp forehead. Her elbow still tingled from brushing his sloping shoulder like an invisible tattoo.

God, his tattoo.

The illicit realization that, all this time, it had lived just beneath the fabric of his perfectly tailored shirts. And now she bore knowledge of his body that her co-workers at Kane Foods did not.

The drive was mostly silent, broken only by Mason's occasional instructions to take this exit or that turn until he pointed to a glittering high-rise.

"Here we are," he said.

Charlotte applied as much effort to keeping her jaw from dropping open at the sight of Mason's Walnut Street condo in Rittenhouse Square as she had to pretending that piloting his Aston hadn't terrified her.

They pulled up to the valet station before the fourteen-story building with long, clean lines, exposed steel beams and the broad expanses of glass on every level reflecting smears of colored light from the city.

Charlotte put the car in Park but left it running, unbuckling her seat belt and grabbing her purse before stepping out as soon as the attendant opened her door. She sucked in a deep breath of night air, forcing the dizzying scents of leather and Mason Kane from her lungs.

They had spoken little on the drive, as if the tension in the elevator had followed them into the equally close quarters of the car, neither of them willing to break the silence with idle chatter.

With a practiced flourish, the smooth-faced kid peeked into the back seat and, spotting the garment bag, handed it off to Mason, who already had his duffel bag slung over his shoulder.

The attendant slid behind the wheel, and the Aston purred off.

Charlotte and Mason stood facing each other, the summer heat still radiating up from the sidewalk, the sultry breath of a coming storm sifting through their hair.

Now.

Now was the moment when she would pull out her phone, bring up the ride app. Bid him goodnight. If she did this, the past three hours could be bundled into a box neither of them would ever have to open again. He might smile at her secretively every now and then. Wink at her in acknowledgment, but that would be the end of it.

If she left now.

"Come up," he said.

It wasn't question. It wasn't even an invitation.

It was an answer.

An answer to her own admission in the elevator. That she liked looking at him. That she could look at him more if she wanted.

That he wanted her to.

"Okay," she said.

Together they entered a foyer that rivaled the soaring marble lobby of the Kane Foods headquarters and passed a sprawling security desk. A guard who might only be moonlighting from his regular job as a Navy SEAL nodded to them.

"Good evening, Mr. Kane."

"Hey, Lou." Mason thumped the sleek glass surface of the desk as he passed. "When are you going to start calling me Mason like I've asked?"

"Next time, Mr. Kane," Lou said with the fond familiarity of a well-worn ritual.

Charlotte's heels echoed like gunshots as they approached the gleaming gold doors of an elevator, her stomach flipping when they opened with a musical *ting*.

The couple who spilled out could have stepped right from the pages an ad for couture, trailing the scents of expensive perfume and cigar smoke in their wake. The man leaned into his partner, whispering something that made her cackle like a witch as they drifted toward the broad glass doors.

Mason motioned to the luxe wood-paneled cube the couple had just vacated. "After you."

With her heart beating in her throat, Charlotte stepped in and watched as he flashed a silvery card at a small sensor before pushing the button for the top floor.

The ride was silent, smooth and quick, Charlotte's stomach rising into her throat when the elevator glided to a stop.

When the doors opened, they exited directly into the penthouse.

Because of course he'd have the penthouse.

Two years into her role as executive assistant to Parker Kane, Charlotte had thought herself immune to the kind of openmouthed wonder wealth often experienced by those not accustomed to it. The yachts, the private jets, the country estates and resorts. She was always adjacent to these things. Near them, but not *part* of them.

Standing in the entryway of Mason Kane's private residence, looking at the glittering Philadelphia skyline through his floor-to-ceiling windows, she couldn't help but feel a stab of wonder.

To *live* like this.

To have this as the backdrop when you ate dinner, took phone calls, watched TV.

She couldn't even begin to process it.

Mason slung his duffel bag down by the door and hooked the clothes hanger on the vertical handle of what she assumed was a coat closet.

"Make yourself at home," he said, stepping out of his sneakers.

Charlotte almost laughed. As if she, Charlotte Westbrook, public school–educated daughter of a schoolteacher and steel-mill worker, could *ever* feel at home in a place like this.

In a nod to physical comfort, she removed her heels and parked them beneath the lacquered black entryway table before placing her purse on top of it. She quickly opened it and checked her phone when Mason disappeared through a door off the main hallway.

She had six texts and two missed calls from Jamie.

Report?

Seriously, bitch. Spill it.

I will only forgive you for not answering me if you are literally having sex with him right now.

Okay, but really. Do I need to call the police? Because I will.

PS. If you don't answer me in the next thirty minutes, I'm using that picture I took of you after you peed your pants at Storybook Land for your missing poster.

CHARLIE Text. Me. Back.

Shaking her head fondly, she tapped out a quick reply. Doing fine, JAMES. Will fill you in later. Don't wait up.

Mason reemerged, shirtless, barefoot and wearing dove-gray sweatpants that worshipped the rounded globes of an ass Charlotte had oft admired in his tailored slacks, which didn't fit him half this well.

"Drink?" he asked, sauntering toward the living room.

Charlotte steadied herself against the table. She didn't need a drink. She needed a priest.

On a shaky inhale, she checked her reflection in the mirror above the entryway table and attempted to smooth down a few wiry hairs the breeze had ruffled.

Nothing for it now.

The marble floors were cool beneath her bare feet as she walked toward the living room, her breath catching as she saw the angular Art Deco spires of the Liberty Place skyscrapers puncturing the night sky through the south bank of windows.

She had to admit, she'd speculated in the past about what Mason Kane's residence might look like, but her fantasies had missed the mark entirely. In her mind, he spent his evenings lolling resplendently in an upscale but perpetually cluttered man cave, fitted out with a large-screen TV, top-of-the-line sound system, lots of rich wood paneling, leather couches, well-stocked wet bar.

Maybe a stripper pole for special occasions.

The wet bar she had been correct about. But it wasn't the vintage *Mad Men*–esque brass-and-wood affair she'd had in mind. It was a simple nook off a kitchen that opened onto the main living space. Chrome appliances. Black marble countertops. Clean white cupboards. The theme continued in the living room. Long, deep-seated couches the gray of thunderclouds dotted with simple throw pillows of black and white. Glass coffee table. Large gas fireplace with an elegant white mantel. Zen-like abstract art.

Not austere, but pure. Serene. Almost monkish in its simplicity.

"What'll it be?" Mason stood with his broad, bare back to her, a symphony of muscles tensing as he opened a bottle of scotch and poured himself a generous three-finger serving.

Charlotte bit her lip and sat down on one of the white leather stools in front of the kitchen island. "Bourbon. With a rock, if you have it."

He cast a curious look at her over the shoulder covered by the smoky swirls of his tattoo.

"I've never seen you drink bourbon at the many and various Kane Foods executive events and ass-kissing shindigs."

"You've never seen me drink, period," Charlotte said, tracing a silvery vein in the black marble with her finger.

"I seem to recall you with glass in hand on several occasions." He bent to a minifridge beneath the counter and pulled out a brushed-metal ice cube tray. The rolling slopes of his arms flexed as the tray cracked and he dropped a perfect glacial cube into a rocks glass.

"Club soda," she said, resisting the urge to fan her feverish cheeks while his back was still to her. "No way would I introduce any kind of judgment-impairing substance to an equation that includes Parker Kane."

Mason chuffed in agreement, taking a step back to examine the backlit bottles lining the shelves above the bar.

"Speaking of my father, did you know he's looking at adding a distillery to his collection?" he asked.

"I did," she said, having been copied on a good deal of the correspondence flying back and forth between Parker Kane and Laurent Renaud of 4 Thieves. Judging by the latter's terse one-sentence responses, negotiations weren't going especially well.

Mason turned toward to her, biting his full lower lip as he caressed her with an assessing look. "What do I want you to taste?"

Like. Charlotte's mind appended this unspoken word to his question.

"I'm not picky," she said, wanting to puncture a hole in the unbearable, maddening tension building with each passing second.

Because wasn't that what *she* was doing here? Wasn't that what *they* were doing here?

"I know just the thing." After scanning the shelves, he brought down a Willett Family Estate Fifteen-Year Straight Bourbon Whiskey—which she knew sold in the neighborhood of seven thousand dollars.

"No, no, no," she insisted. "You don't need to do that—"

"I'm not going to." He crossed to the island and placed the bottle and glass before her. A sly smile tugged at one corner of his mouth. "You are."

She shook her head violently. "This is absolutely ridiculous."

"What's absolutely ridiculous is you sending bottle after bottle of this to my father's many cronies but never getting to try it yourself." He pushed it toward her.

His words poked a bruise she hadn't known she was

hiding. The countless hours, days, weeks, months spent in service of a man who never hesitated to point out her mistakes but hadn't parted with a single thank-you. The grueling effort of making his life easier by making hers harder. The nights she spent twisted into an anxious ball just so men would never know or care how much effort was required to organize events where they could eat canapés and feel lordly with each other.

"Pour." He paired the order with a look more direct and commanding than she would have known him capable of until this moment.

The bottle was cool and silky in her hands as she eased the cork out with a friendly squeak. She carefully tipped amber liquid over the already-melting ice cube, stopping when it was half submerged.

Mason lifted his glass of scotch in invitation, and she clinked hers against it, immeasurably grateful her hands didn't shake as she brought it to her lips and sipped.

Her eyes flew wide as her palate exploded with a bouquet of flavors she didn't even known were possible. To her, bourbon had always tasted like...bourbon. She quickly scanned the immediate vicinity. Searching for anything to write with and finding nothing, she set her drink down and sprinted to get her phone with a quick "excuse me" flung after her.

"What is it?" Mason asked, his forehead creased in concern. "Are you okay?"

"Absolutely," Charlotte said when she returned. "I just need to get this description before I forget." She trained her attention downward as she frantically typed, blood orange, dark chocolate, oak, warmed prunes, nutmeg, perique tobacco, stewed cherry.

"Sorry." She took another sip of her drink, her eyes falling closed as she sifted for any small detail she might have missed. When she opened them again, Mason was beside her, a bemused smile on his face, the naked skin of his torso radiating body heat and a blend of scents as delicious as the bourbon.

Smoky scotch, clean sweat, fabric softener, the ghost of the aftershave he must have applied that morning.

She had forgotten how to breathe.

How often had she tried to capture this exact feeling? The sick, glad, dizzy anticipation of the imminent *what next?*

Mason took another sip of his scotch and set it on the counter. "I have a proposition," he said.

Charlotte followed suit, relishing the way the liquor became a velvet burn all the way to her belly. "What's that?"

"You're writing about a world you've never lived in. You're just taking your notes and trying to imagine what it's really like."

She wiped a bead of sweat from her glass. "That's pretty much how research works."

Mason's eyes were the color of seawater shot through with sunshine beneath half-lowered lids. His fingers closed over her hand, and he tugged her to her feet.

She stood before him, so close she couldn't bear it. Couldn't bear the washboard of his tensed abdominals and his flat, small belly button and the abrupt clefts of his hipbones and the dangerous wedges of muscle that disappeared below the waistband of his sweatpants.

The reality of a man she had fantasized about for nights on end. So near. So alive.

"Let me *show* you the inside," he said. "One week in Côte d'Azur. You, me and paradise."

Are you mad? was the immediate answer that arrived in her mind. One she might have spoken aloud, were it not for the way he studied her.

Intently.

Carefully.

Like he'd *thought* about this.

"You can't be serious," she said.

Mason cocked his head. "That's a common misconception."

"I mean it." Setting her glass aside, Charlotte tried to stitch together the pieces of her tattered resolve. "Despite your reputation, you of all people should understand how dangerous that could be. We *work* together. At a company owned by your father. Who is strenuously opposed to any kind of *personal* encounters between employees."

"What do you call this?" His broad shoulders rounded toward her as he obliterated another half inch of the space between them. "You. Here. Alone with me?"

Fair question, that. One Charlotte had asked herself on the drive over. One she still couldn't fully answer.

"You want to know what I think?" he asked.

"Sometimes," she admitted.

"Part of you wants to break my father's rules."

Want.

Why did that word glow like a banked coal when he said it? Why did it eat up what remained of the oxygen her shallow breaths afforded her?

"Even though my entire livelihood depends on him?"

Mason moved closer still. "*Because* your entire livelihood depends on him. My father is an infuriatingly demanding human and putting up with him is exhausting."

Charlotte hadn't expected him to hit so close to the mark.

Bone-tired and soul-weary from trying to keep up with his rigorous and never-ending standards of excellence, she dragged herself through each week. Trying, trying, and every day falling a little further behind. As if some part of her had gone on strike. Digging its heels in, setting its jaw, refusing to cooperate until conditions improved.

They never had.

They never would.

"So my being here tonight is, what?" She scoffed. "Some feeble act of rebellion?"

"I prefer to think of it as an act of bravery."

His eyes dropped to her mouth.

Then Mason Kane touched her.

A hand placed along the length of her jaw, index finger in the dip below her ear, thumb on her cheekbone, his breath warm on her face. And she had no choice but to look at him. To absorb the intense, baking heat of his regard.

"You are more than just my father's executive assistant, Charlotte. Just like I'm more than the chief marketing officer of my father's company. And that more? That's how we ended up running into each other tonight. Of all the places in Philadelphia either of us could be tonight, we were there. Together."

Her book. His League.

The intersection of two distinctly non-corporate dreams.

Both with an element of risk.

Risk like accepting Mason's invitation to come up. *Eagerly* accepting, in fact.

Like it or not, she had welcomed the danger. Had even been more than a little turned on by it. Intrigued by the prospect of what might happen between them if she did.

"One week," Mason said again, pulling her from her tangle of thoughts. "You'll be a writer. I'll be your playboy. No expectations. No rules."

Her head swam under his burning, hooded gaze. "There are always rules," she whispered.

His hand slid from her jaw, his fingers delving into the hair at the base of her neck and gently gripping a fistful. His stubble-roughened cheek grazed hers, his lips hot against her ear. "I'll help you break them."

Decadent, drugging heaviness gathered in her navel, her nipples painfully, deliciously hard against her lacy bra.

"I'll think about it," she said.

"Yes." Mason's lips hovered over hers, so close she could taste the scotch. "You will."

He brushed his lips over her jaw, her temple, the hollow below her ear, traced the lobe and teased the shell with quick flicks of his tongue before lighting it up with a gentle exhale that sent her into a full-body shiver.

An answering rumble vibrated through his chest as he explored the sensitive skin of her neck, pausing to taste her, to suck and nip until she was half-mad with need.

"Do you want me to kiss you, Charlotte?" he asked darkly.

"Yes," she sighed, a one-syllable surrender.

Only then did he claim her mouth. Branding her with his lips, sweeping his hot, smoky tongue over hers. Drinking from her, their teeth scraping as he gripped her waist with his free hand and curled his hips into hers in a slow, undulating wave.

She felt him against her stomach, steely beneath the fabric of his sweatpants.

He broke the kiss, leaving her panting and dazed.

Goose flesh prickled her scalp as Mason tightened his grip on her hair, tilting her head back so she was looking up into his scalding gaze.

"You can touch me," he rasped.

Until that moment, Charlotte hadn't realized her arms hung limp at her sides.

Hesitant, her mouth still burning, she brought her hands to his torso, marveling at the foreign feel of him beneath her palms. The smooth and hard slopes of his muscle, the faint pulse of his heartbeat underneath. She trailed her fingertips to the dip of his sternum before letting them ride over the ridges of his abdominal muscles, which tightened under her touch. She traced the skin just above his waistband, a thrill sparking through her when he shuddered and groaned a rough, low *unh*.

Mason sucked in a quick breath and jerked his hips back.

"Not yet." His voice was hoarse as he moved her hand away.

He led her to the living room, where he backed her up against the south-facing windows. Never taking his eyes off her, he walked backward and seated himself on a chair opposite, his posture a cocky slouch, his knees wide, long arms draped arrogantly over the sides as he swept her with a leisurely stare.

It was the kind of tableau a man with billions of dollars at his disposal can orchestrate for his own pleasure. A woman and the city he played like hell's own harp.

Charlotte had been many things in her twenty-seven years, but *watched* was not one of them. Not like this.

Not by a man like Mason Kane.

Heady, this feeling. His awareness becoming hers. Seeing herself through his eyes. No part of her remaining untouched, uncontained by his attention.

"Take off your dress," he ordered.

Such a mundane process, and one she had performed thousands of times, was somehow made new and strangely illicit by the simple act of his having commanded her to do it. With trembling fingers, she reached behind her and pulled down the zipper, shrugging off both straps and lowering it over her bra.

"Slower," he said.

Obediently, she worked it unhurriedly down her ribs, slithering it over her hips, bending to draw it down her thighs, her knees, her calves before stepping out of it.

"Now touch yourself."

She hesitated, her ever-present self-consciousness sending up a flare of alarm.

"Touch. Yourself." Mason slouched down farther in the chair, his hand running over the bulge in his sweatpants and slowing to grip it. "Show me how you like it."

Just as she saw herself through his eyes, she now felt herself with his hands. Conjuring his roughened palms to glide down over her belly, to cup her through the thin, lacy panties, already damp with desire.

Mason's guttural grunt resonated deep within her belly as he lifted his hand and bit his knuckle, the look on his face nothing short of feral.

With his fevered look blazing into her, she began to explore her slick folds.

Mason rose from his chair and stalked over to her, one hand gently gripping her neck, the other brushing hers aside so her could take over what she'd begun.

She gasped, her palms flat against the window for support.

His mouth was at her ear, his fingers slipping in and out of her, coating the electric bundle of nerves at the apex of her sex. "You're very wet, Charlotte."

A strangled moan was her only reply.

"Who made you wet?" he asked.

"You," she breathed.

"Who?" he repeated, increasing the pressure on her aching nub.

"You did."

"Good girl." He lowered his head and circled her nipple through the lace of her bra with the tip of his tongue, all the while toying with her in that maddeningly lazy loop.

She writhed against him, burning, restless, hungry. Ready.

Releasing her neck, Mason pulled the cup of her bra down and sucked her nipple into his mouth, testing the pearly tip with his teeth.

Charlotte lost herself to a stunned, carnal cry of pure pleasure. She was ecstasy-drunk. Drowning. Losing herself.

Then he was on his knees before her, dragging her

panties down her legs and putting his mouth where his hand had been. Licking and flicking her swollen flesh, stopping when she was on the edge of beyond to tease her with the flat of his tongue. A deepening current rode down the insides of her thighs and to the soles of her feet, cycling back to the molten nexus building at her center.

Mason fastened his lips over her, sucking and humming as he slapped her ass with a stinging blow that sent her shooting straight into the stratosphere.

Charlotte surrendered to it all. To the mingling of pleasure and pain. To the unbearably intense clenching threatening to turn her inside out. To her knees dissolving into sand and Mason catching her as she folded over him, her cheek resting against his back.

In a move that stole her breath, he pushed himself to his feet with her slung over his shoulder, caveman style.

Too weak and pleasure-slack to raise any objections, Charlotte allowed herself to be carried down the hall and to his bedroom, where he slung her onto his bed. The covers were silky beneath her back, Mason a blue-black outline against the backdrop of the city lights, which glittered like a carpet of scattered stars.

Crawling to the edge of the bed, she knelt, finding the waistband of his sweatpants and pulling them down.

He was naked beneath.

Charlotte ran her fingers over his cock. Hot as a branding iron and hard as steel, velvety beneath her grip.

"Spit on it," he said.

Heat flooded her cheeks. Bringing her mouth close

enough to feel the heat of his arousal on her lips, she did as instructed.

"Do you want it?" Mason asked, his voice barbed with desire as he began moving his hand up and down his own length.

She didn't just want it. She *needed* it. Needed to feel him inside her like her lungs needed air. To be filled, to be relieved of an all-consuming, suffocating lack.

"Yes."

"Then tell me."

A fresh wave of lust flowed into her, gathering as a pleasant weight in her still-burning core.

"I want it," she said, all traces of restraint long since incinerated.

"And you can have it." Mason bent and pulled up his sweatpants. "When you come to Côte d'Azur with me."

Five

I want it.

Mason had replayed these words in his head over and over, mentally slowing them down to savor every syllable.

Charlotte had meant it.

Remembering the way her freckle-dappled body had writhed on his silky black comforter, he felt the vice-like grip of desire.

The spice of her arousal still haunted his tongue. The feel of her fingernails still scored his scalp. Her lush, feminine cry as she came still echoed in ears.

He wanted to make her do it again.

And again.

Madness, to think of the hungry way she had stared at his erection. Madness, what he had said when she did.

When you come to Côte d'Azur with me.

Mason had never been as dedicated to the art of navel gazing as his twin, but his spur of the moment decision to invite Charlotte Westbrook to accompany him to the French Riviera had given him pause.

Impulsive. Impetuous. Reckless.

Words that had trailed him like smoke for as long as he could remember.

They somehow took on sharper edges when in proximity to her.

When it came to potential romantic partners, Mason knew he was perhaps the worst possible choice for her in terms of long-term stability.

But stability wasn't what she lacked.

Their hours together last night had demonstrated that just as clearly as it had revealed how much she longed for freedom. Adventure. Inspiration.

The idea that, even for one week, Mason could give her a world she'd never experienced without destroying the one she already had?

This proposition had proved too tempting to pass up, despite the risks.

Or perhaps, because of them.

Stealing his father's executive assistant away was a gamble, yes.

One he badly needed to win.

Because seeing her face in the crowd at The League had woken something in him Mason couldn't put back to sleep. Something he craved to taste more of.

But just as The League had given him an outlet for the simmering rage he could no longer chase away with reliable distractions, delayed gratification had restored a measure of excitement Mason's life had begun to lose.

Though he had showered, shaved and dressed himself in freshly pressed slacks and shirt, he could still feel her on his skin. He'd spent the long, sleepless night imagining how she would look when he saw her this morning. Whether she'd be more or less likely to meet his eye after what had happened between them.

Less, he decided.

And he was right.

Though not for the reasons he expected.

He exited the elevator on the executive floor of the Kane Foods International office, a cardboard coffee cup in his hand and an uncommon ripple of anticipation in his stomach.

Charlotte's desk was at the end of a broad corridor, the double doors of his father's office behind her. Mason often wondered if his father had arranged this on purpose. So that she would have to sit with her back to him, never knowing when he might pop up and look over her shoulder.

He suspected the answer was yes.

She was exactly where she had been every morning since she'd started with Kane Foods two years ago, but the sight of her this morning felt new and wonderfully strange. Having seen her as she was last night, every detail of her appearance now screamed control. Precision. Self-discipline.

The tightly wound bun. The fully buttoned blouse. The glasses. The muted makeup. Like a cage for the wild creature he had witnessed. One that had to be contained. Controlled. Tamed.

He cleared his throat, waiting for her to look up him.

"Good morning," she said, with a neutral formality that alarmed and perplexed him.

"My night was better," he replied, carefully observing her face for any noticeable change.

She didn't smile. Didn't look away. Didn't even blush. *Shit*.

"I'm very glad to hear that," she said in her smoothly curated telephone voice. "Just a heads-up, the executive huddle has been moved to ten. I'll be sending an update shortly."

He felt like a man drowning. Was her stiff decorum an overcorrection for last night? An act in case they were being observed? An amnesiac rebuke? Some sort of shy-girl performance art?

With growing dread, he realized he had absolutely no clue how to read Charlotte Westbrook.

"Is everything…okay?" As he asked this, he tried to say with his eyes what he couldn't with his mouth.

"Of course," she said coolly. "Why wouldn't it be?"

"You just seem…different today," Mason said.

"Do I?" She sounded guileless and surprised.

Just as he began to wonder if last night had been some sort of head trauma–induced hallucination, he spotted a small smudge on her neck where thick concealer interrupted the field of her pale freckles.

Charlotte tugged at her collar, noticing the direction of his glance.

Mason set his coffee down and leaned on the counter. "Charlotte," he said, dropping to a conspiratorial volume. "If it was something I did—" he cleared his throat "—or *didn't* do, I am more than happy to rectify the situation by any means necessary."

"Not at all," she replied. It was that same polite dismissal she'd used via IM yesterday. "I really shouldn't keep you. Your guest is waiting in your office whenever you're ready."

"Guest?" Ice water spilled down his spine. "But I'm not expecting anyone until my eleven o'clock."

Charlotte offered no further information. Only faced him with the dispassionate but expectant blankness he'd seen on countless occasions when people made their way to this counter to make demands of her time.

He stalked away, hating himself for the bubble of hope he felt when she called after him. It promptly burst when he saw her standing, holding out his coffee cup.

Deciding that telling her to toss it would reveal more than he was willing to part with, he wordlessly returned and took it from her, miserable that the accidental brush of her fingertip sent a tingle shooting all the way to his elbow.

When he opened his office door with his free hand, Mason saw his guest, and everything made instant, terrible sense.

Madison Bradford.

Madison Bradford, whom he had brought as a date to many Kane Foods social functions.

Madison Bradford, with whom he had been photographed at operas, concerts and charity balls.

Madison Bradford, who was dramatically draped over the arm of the leather couch in the corner of his office. A former model, her elegant thoroughbred form had been featured in the perfumed pages of *Vogue* and *Marie Claire*, her specialty a beautifully broken and fragile malaise. Once represented by Ford, she liked to tell anyone who would listen that she'd aged out at twenty-five, though Mason suspected it had more to do with a famously mercurial temperament.

Though her modeling days were many years past, Madison still had an old family name and the money to match, and she liked to remind people of both facts.

She didn't rise when she saw him, ensuring he had ample time to appreciate the long lines of her body in its clingy, sleeveless knit dress with geometric patterns that complimented her angular frame.

"There he is." Madison had the breathy voice of a silver screen starlet and a smile that didn't quite make it to her eyes. "The man who kept me waiting."

Mason set his coffee and laptop bag down on the desk and glanced at his phone. Seven forty-five a.m. He couldn't remember when he'd last been on time—early, even—and told himself it had been his inability to sleep, not his eagerness to see Charlotte that had propelled him out of bed in the gray predawn light.

"It couldn't have been for long," he said.

"It's been months," she purred, rising to her wickedly sharp heels. Designer, like her purse, her dress, her jewelry…her life. "Since you've forgotten how to answer my calls, I thought a little visit might be in order."

Mason hung his suit jacket on the coatrack, which, like his desk, his meeting table, his couch and the priceless antiques adorning his office, had been chosen by his father's decorator. "This isn't exactly the ideal spot for a reunion," he said, seating himself in the leather wingback chair behind his desk.

Madison sauntered toward him, her artfully enhanced lips pushed out in a pout. The effect was ludicrous against the backdrop of her razor cheekbones, sky-blue eyes and chic helmet of golden hair. "Are you saying you're not happy to see me?"

Reaching into his bag, he extracted his laptop and set it on the docking station. "I'm saying I don't have *time* to see you. My first meeting is in fifteen minutes."

A blatant lie.

She sidled up beside him and seated herself on his desk, swiveling her bare knees against his arm, her heels dangling near the seat of his chair. "I seem to remember you could do a lot for a girl in fifteen minutes."

"Madison," he said, trying to sound gentle. "This isn't a good time."

She picked up the sleek black remote at the edge of his desk with manicured hands, pressing the button that turned the glass front wall of his office opaque. "It also isn't the first time," she said.

Despite his deliberate effort not to do so, he found himself comparing. Madison's possessive stare to Charlotte's shy glance. Her tawny, artificially tanned limbs to Charlotte's soft, pale, freckled legs.

One of her heels fell to the carpet, and she slid her bare foot into his lap, stroking him with her toes. "Remember what I did to you under the table at the Met Gala?"

Mason shoved her foot out of his crotch, but not before his door swung open to reveal Charlotte standing there with a stack of papers in her arms.

In all the time she had worked at Kane Foods, she had never once entered his office without knocking and had never even dared to knock when his privacy screen was on.

"These need your signature." Her expression stony, she marched forward and thumped the stack on his desk before turning on her heel and leaving without so much as a hello.

A smile tugged at his lips despite the damning circumstances she'd found him in.

It was an uncharacteristically bold and confrontational move on Charlotte's part.

Progress.

When he snapped back to attention, he noticed that Madison, too, had watched her go.

"Oh, Mason." Her hand landed on his forearm as she gave him a throaty laugh. *"Her?"*

The ever-present hot blue pilot flame at the base of his skull flickered to vibrant, destructive life.

"Her *what*?" he demanded.

"You ignore me for months on end, feed me bullshit excuses about needing to focus on your training for *her*?" Her dusky chuckle became a shrill cackle.

Mason shook his arm from beneath her pointed grip. "You don't know anything about her."

"You're right." Madison shifted her hips to the center of the desk and lifted her leg to straddle his chair. The hem of her dress rode up her long, lean thighs, and he saw she wore nothing beneath. "But I know things about you."

"Please leave." His scarred knuckles whitened as he gripped the arms of his chair. "Now."

Ignoring him, she trailed a finger over her knee and up her bare thigh. "I know that you need someone who can take it as hard as you need to give it."

"What I need," he said, pushing her knees together, "is for you to get off my desk."

"She's not like us, Mason." Madison pressed a cold palm to his jaw. "She doesn't know the pressure we face. Or what it's like to be raised by someone who thinks of you as a chess piece or a bartering chip."

"If you *really* knew me, you wouldn't be justifying your unwanted presence in my office by poking at the psychological trauma of my childhood." Pushing his chair back, Mason stood.

"Why don't you ask her to join us sometime?" Madison scooted to the edge of the desk, kicking her legs like a lazy swimmer. "Then we can ruin a fresh-faced ingenue together. Like old times."

Just as he had with Charlotte earlier that morning, Mason felt he was seeing Madison for the first time.

Beautiful, yes. But bored, jaded and sadistic. He would sooner walk into the Delaware River than deliver Charlotte into Madison's pointed claws.

Charlotte, who believed in happily-ever-afters.

Charlotte, who had looked at him with curiosity instead of ownership.

Charlotte, who could be hurt. Who *had* been hurt.

This fact more than any other stirred the sludge of worry in his gut.

"If you won't leave, I will," he said, brushing past her.

"I won't be ignored, Mason." She clutched his biceps as she drew herself to her full, offended height. "I *won't* be ignored, Mason."

He gave her an ugly smile. "So it's threats?" Mason leaned closer to her, his lips near her diamond-studded ear. "One call from me, and the name Madison Bradford will be a joke they tell at the parties you're no longer invited to."

Her eyes were glassy with rage, her perfect white teeth shining in a rictus grin. "This discussion isn't over."

"Maybe not." He shrugged her hand off his arm and strode toward the door, waiting until she stiffly gathered her purse and marched past him down the hallway and to the elevator. "But we are."

When she was gone, he walked straight to Charlotte's desk, "Get up," he said.

Her insistently stoic expression slipped from its moorings. "Excuse me?"

"You're coming with me. Now." He started toward the hallway leading to the Kane family's private wing of the executive floor.

"But I'm not allowed—"

"You are if I say you are."

Hesitantly, she stood and stepped out from behind her desk, her eyes nervously flicking from his father's closed office doors down the hall.

Mason took her by the hand and tugged her in his wake through the private wing, noticing how she rapidly scanned the artwork, the furniture, every detail denied her until this moment. As much as he would have loved to watch her face as she registered each new discovery, he had different designs.

He cut a sharp left into the lushly appointed sitting area, the deeply piled carpet making their passage completely silent as he crossed to a door, opened it and locked it behind them once Charlotte was inside.

To call it a bathroom would be largely inaccurate.

Complete with a marble vanity, a steam shower, a sauna and a chaise longue, the Kanes' private restroom was more like a miniature spa.

It was also the only place on the executive floor without security cameras.

Charlotte's lips formed a little O of surprise as she took it all in.

"Ridiculous, isn't it?" he said, picking up a gilded tissue box holder and setting it roughly down with a disgusted snort.

"Why did you bring me here?" She folded her arms across breasts he tried not to think about having his mouth on less than ten hours ago.

"So we could have a little talk about what happened out there this morning." He leaned back against the vanity, placing his hands on the smooth marble so he didn't place them on her smooth skin.

Charlotte's wide chocolaty eyes fell to her shoes as she twisted her slim fingers together. "What happened, was me, coming to my senses. About last night, your offer, all of it."

A flash of anxiety tightened his stomach. Until that moment, he hadn't realized how much her answer mattered to him. "Because Madison Bradford showed up at my office uninvited?"

Charlotte sighed and seated herself on the chaise. She looked utterly, completely, ludicrously at home against the backdrop of luxury she'd been denied by his father's arbitrary dictates. She was at once finer and more lovely than anything that had been expertly curated in this room.

"It's not just Madison Bradford," she said. "It's the never-ending parade of *lady friends* and *gal pals* dangling from your arm on Page Six."

"I had no idea you were paying such close attention to my extracurricular activities," he said, oddly flattered.

At this, that much-beloved flush returned to her cheeks, and Mason felt an inexplicable rush of gratitude.

"You're right," she said. "It's absolutely no business of mine who you choose to sleep with or when. I just know I'm not cut out to be one of them."

Bedrock, at last.

"Charlotte, there is no *them*," he said. "There hasn't been in months. Not since I started The League."

Her brow creased in confusion. "But I've seen you. All the events. The dinners."

"Appearances. And yes, I have—" he paused, searching for the least contentious word "—*satisfied* some of them in other ways."

"Like you satisfied *Daddy's secretary*?" The bitter, scornful look on her face approximated Madison's expression so precisely that he had to fight to suppress a shudder.

"I may be inexperienced, Mason, but I'm not naive. Women like Madison are your entrée. Forgive me for not wanting to be your palate cleanser."

He was across the room in a flash, standing before the chaise, frustration throbbing like a sick migraine in his skull. Frustration, he realized, primarily with himself. Because he had earned his reputation. Had constructed it from the ground up. Mason Kane, the playboy heir to a billion-dollar empire. Shallow. Arrogant. Indulgent.

Who could blame her for believing what he'd so carefully built?

"That's not why I want you to come to the Côte d'Azur with me," he insisted.

She searched his face as if looking for an answer before her question was even spoken. "Then why do you?"

In this lushly ostentatious room, Mason stripped himself of all artifice, crouching down to bring his face level with hers.

"Because watching you try seven-thousand dollar bourbon was like tasting it for the first time," he said. "Because for at least one week of my life, I want to give back some of what working for my father has taken from you. Because I'm a selfish bastard and last night is the most real I've felt in the last two years, and I want this. I want this, and I will do everything in my power to prevent any consequences from landing on your doorstep. *If* this is something you want, too."

He stood there in swarming silence, seeing the struggle behind her eyes.

"Is it?" he asked, painfully aware of the pleading note coloring the air between them.

Six

Charlotte looked at the man before her, his face open and earnest and not resembling the Mason Kane she knew at all.

Want.

That word again.

Was this something she wanted?

Of course.

Of course she wanted to leap into a private jet and be whisked away to the French Riviera by the gorgeous, seductive, charismatic man she'd worshipped from afar for the last two years.

That didn't stop an endless array of possible complications from lining up like roadblocks in her head.

Her mother had been the first added to her mental list, only to have it rapidly removed by Jamie, who had busted her, and hard, waiting on the couch when she had crept in after 1:00 a.m. She had parted with as many details about the evening as she could and was rewarded with her brother nearly shaking the teeth out of her head and asking her if she was out of her Diet-Coke addled mind when she told him she intended to refuse.

He'd insisted that he and Gail could cover their mother's care and that everything would be fine.

Charlotte was surprised by just how badly she'd wanted this to be true.

Truly, she had decided how she would answer before she came to work this morning. Or thought she had, until the arrival of Madison Bradford.

As Charlotte had sat, forcing herself to move through her morning routine of bringing Parker Kane his coffee and running him through his schedule for the day, she couldn't help but be aware of the other woman's presence, pulsing in her peripheral consciousness. A convenient placeholder for a long train of names and faces, of which Charlotte's only distinction was "most recent."

She hadn't been prepared for the jealousy this thought would produce, bubbling up inside her like hot tar. The old, familiar feelings of insecurity, worry, neediness it woke within her psyche.

"Well?" Mason asked, laying the question at her feet once more.

Despite all that had happened, all that *could* happen, her answer was the same.

Charlotte *did* want it.

She wanted it more than anything in recent or distant memory.

"Even if I did want to go," she said. "There's no guarantee your father would give me the time off."

"My father may pay you for your time, but he doesn't *own* you, Charlotte. Five days off is not an unreasonable request when you haven't taken a vacation in two years." Mason's expression had softened, perhaps encouraged by her use of the conditional.

"I wasn't aware you were paying such close attention to my extracurricular activities," she said, triumphantly flinging his own line back at him.

"One week." Mason captured the hand she had been wringing. "That's all I'm asking. I'll take care of everything. You just have to pack your bag and *come*."

Lord knew Mason Kane could ensure the last part of that sentence. Charlotte could barely meet her own eye in the mirror this morning remembering some of the things she'd done and said under his command.

Unable to think with him in such close proximity, she rose and began to pace. Turning things over in her head one last time.

Mason stood as well, waiting her out. The darkening of a bruise was barely visible at one corner of his mouth. At some point after she'd left his apartment in a lather, he must have used wound sealant to knit his eyebrow together.

Charlotte had spent so much time looking at him, but had to wonder how many other details she had missed.

Was she really prepared to miss so many more? To let her typical, unfailing practicality steal days of sun and turquoise water, nights with the salt air on her neck? And Mason Kane. His eyes, his hands, his mouth. This man she had quietly worshipped, fantasized about, wanted, *wanted* when now he wanted her, too.

"Okay," she said with a decisive nod.

Mason's eyes lit up, and boyish excitement stripped years from his face. "You'll go?" he asked, as if he didn't trust that he'd heard her right.

"On one condition," she said, privately amused when his grin faltered.

"What's that?" he asked.

"You know the blue tie with the tiny diamonds? The one you wore to the president's club banquet?"

His brows knit together. "Yeah."

"Bring it with you."

He planted a hand on the small of her back and pulled her body against his. "Charlotte Westbrook, I don't know if a single soul in this office knows who you really are."

Charlotte wasn't sure she did, either.

She made herself put her hands on his arms, feeling the gradients of muscle beneath the fine fabric of his shirt. If she was doing this—*really* doing this—she needed to get used to touching him. Casually. Intentionally. Purposefully.

His hand moved lower, his palm sliding over the curve of her behind. "Do you have any idea how badly I want you right now?"

"Some," she said, feeling him growing hard against her belly.

"Good." Mason skimmed her mouth with the tip of his index finger.

Surprising even herself, she closed her lips over it, tracing the ridges of his fingerprint with her tongue. Pleased when his eyes widened before his lids went slack and hazy.

"Christ," he whispered.

Charlotte pressed it in farther, taking it until she could feel it at the back of her throat.

She swallowed.

Mason groaned as he pulled his finger out with an audible pop. He looked at it, wet and glistening with a red ring of her lipstick around the base that he didn't wipe away.

"We leave tomorrow," he said. "I'll be at your house by noon."

Saturday.

Which would mean she needed to tell Parker Kane today.

Now, she thought, while the excitement of the moment hadn't yet been gnawed away by more what-ifs and shoulds.

"I'll be ready."

"You'd better be." His fingertips flexed against her ass, grinding her against him one last time before he set her free.

Charlotte unlocked the door and held it open.

"You go ahead," he said, a sheepish smile lifting the corners of his lips. "I'm going to need a minute."

Judging by the shape pressing against the fabric of his pants, he was going to need several.

"You could just…" She raised her eyebrows and cast a teasing look at the gilded tissue holder.

Mason leaned in close, gently pulling her ear toward his mouth.

"I haven't let myself come in four months, Charlotte," he ground out. "And when I do, it will be because *you* make me."

What those words did to her.

Her stomach felt heavy, her knees buttery, her joints loose and tingling like the buzz after a first drink. Great wells of warmth spread through her chest, her belly, the juncture of her thighs.

She *wanted* this. Wanted to hear it, and feel it, see it.

"But if you break your drought, where will you find all that pent up rage for The League?" she asked teasingly.

"From the memory of you…" Mason whispered. "On Bentley Drake's arm."

With thought lodged in her ear, Charlotte left him to recover.

Walking down the hallway back to her desk on numb, wooden legs, she forgot to be afraid.

The broad polished wood doors behind her desk were closed, so she rapped her usual *tat-tatta-tat* and waited for permission to enter.

"Come in," Parker barked from the other side.

Charlotte shouldered the door open and entered the inner sanctum.

She couldn't help but remember the first time she'd been shown into this office by the receptionist after interviews with both Samuel and Mason Kane.

Samuel had been the first, and Charlotte had honestly been shocked when she was invited back after their cold, awkward exchange. He had been attractive, of course. Alarmingly so. But in a buttoned-up, completely unapproachable, may-or-may-not-be-obsessive-compulsive type of way.

Then she'd returned for her second interview and met the roguish, winking, smirking Mason.

She couldn't believe they were twins.

Any more than she could believe the silver-haired, stone-faced titan behind the broad expanse of desk was their father.

Parker Kane's office was floor-to-ceiling windows on three sides. As if the city itself were part of the staggering collection of paintings, sculptures and antiques that populated the rest of the space.

He leaned over his leather notebook, his eyes trained on the creamy paper folded open before him. "What is it, Miss Westbrook?"

If only her luck would last.

"I'm terribly sorry to interrupt you," she said, lightly perching in one of the chairs opposite his desk. "But I was wondering if there was any way I might be able to take next week off."

The scratching sound of his pen on the paper died abruptly as his hand froze mid-word.

Preparing herself for the arctic blast of his gaze, she was doubly alarmed at what she read on his face instead.

Concern.

"Is everything all right?" His question produced an instant spike of guilt.

"Yes," Charlotte said. "My mother hasn't been doing so well lately, and my brother came in for a surprise visit."

Not a lie, technically, but somehow that only made her feel twice as terrible for it.

"Is she ill?" He looked at her from beneath the imperious ledge of his iron-gray eyebrows.

A fine film of sweat blossomed beneath her arms, and her palms grew clammy and damp. "She has early onset Alzheimer's."

Such a strange sensation, breaching this boundary

that had walled her private life off from the man whose shadow fell across almost every other aspect of it.

Parker Kane drew in a deep breath, setting his pen aside to give her his full attention.

"I'm on the board of Einstein Medical Center. A friend of mine is the head of the neuropsychology unit. I would be more than happy to make an introduction, if you'd like."

Now Charlotte didn't just feel guilty, she felt like lighting herself on fire and leaping out the twenty-fifth-story window. "That's very kind of you."

He waved a hand as if her gratitude was an irritation. "Take the time you need, Miss Westbrook."

"Are you sure?" She'd blurted the words out before she could stop herself. "It would only be from Monday through Friday of next week, and of course, I'll keep up on email while I'm gone—"

"I'm sure that I can make do with the meager staff available to me." It was the closest thing to a joke Charlotte had ever heard him attempt, and it filled her with florid shame for the circumstances.

"In fact," he continued, picking up his pen and resuming his writing. "You can take the rest of the day, if it would help."

Unease began to reach cold tendrils into her gut. Was this some sort of test? An offer she was meant to refuse? It had been a tactic she'd become intimately acquainted with in the years she'd spent with Trent. Assenting to his suggestions for activities beneficial to her, only to discover by his cold silence she'd chosen incorrectly.

"That's not necessary," she protested, her first attempt at teasing out his motive.

"Family before duty." He rubbed dry, leathery palms together. "Away with you."

She'd been dismissed.

Charlotte rose, gathered her things from her desk and walked out of Kane Foods International.

After a short stroll to the Nineteenth Street station, she glanced at the schedule. Seeing that the next train to the Lansdale stop departed in fifteen minutes, she decided to nip into the small convenience store, where, bypassing the bottled water, she selected a nondiet soda instead.

Vacation, after all.

The cashier gave her a conspiratorial smile as he rung her up.

"Playing hooky?" he asked.

"Maybe I am," she said. Having never skipped school a day in her life, she imagined this must be what it felt like.

Charlotte exited the store and sat on a bench. Sipping a cold soda with the sun on her shoulders, she sent a message to let Mason know, in the vaguest terms possible, that the wheels had been set in motion. Then she tucked her phone away and focused on absorbing every detail of this uncommon experience.

Her world felt strange and illicit in the way it had when she stayed home from school sick as a child and, looking at the clock, imagined her classmates filing into the music room or library, lining up for PE when she was lying on the couch watching cooking shows.

When her phone pinged, she half expected it to be Angela Cheng, her workplace confidante, asking her where the hell she was.

Only, it wasn't.

The text was a number she didn't recognize. Five words, but ominous enough to feel like a cloud skating across the sun.

I know about last night.

The words haunted her, puncturing the balloon of her excitement all the way home.

Jamie, of course, had been elated, then suspicious of her unexpected early arrival.

"I'm going" was all Charlotte said.

He wrapped her in an enthusiastic hug before dragging her back toward her bedroom to help her pack.

She sat on the edge of her bed while he mined her closet, sifting the options into Fucking Never, In the Right Lighting and What Were You Thinking?

"Mmm-hmm," she hummed in answer to a question she hadn't heard while reading the strange text message for the seventy-eighth time.

A coveted 212 Manhattan area code.

Google had produced no results.

"Gonna get laidsville to Charlie, I repeat, come in, Charlie." Jamie snapped his fingers at her.

"I'm sorry," she said, looking up at him. "What was the question?"

"The question *was* whether you thought you would be having any formal dinners, but the question *is* why am I struggling to hold your attention during what should be the most exciting exercise of your life?" Jamie hung a clingy green silk dress over the door of her meager closet and sank down on the bed next to her.

Charlotte pulled up the text message and handed her phone to him.

"What the actual F?" he muttered. "Who sent this to you?"

"I have no idea," she said.

Jamie pushed a fall of fine blond hair out of his eyes. "Do you think it could be a wrong number?"

"It's possible." She shrugged. "But it doesn't *feel* like a wrong number."

"Could it be that Bentley guy?"

That had been Charlotte's first thought as well. "It could be. But why would he be texting me from a different number? Wouldn't he want me to know that *he* knows?"

Her brother folded his arms. "I don't like this."

"Do you think it's a sign?" she asked. "Some kind of *abort mission* signal from the universe?"

"Charlotte Marie Westbrook, I'm desperately heartbroken and need to live vicariously through you, and I don't care if you have an entire squadron of stalkers. You are *going*. Now start helping me pick your clothes."

Her stomach flipped when her phone pinged. With metallic adrenaline in her throat, she looked down and felt a wash of relief when she saw Mason's name.

Thirteen hours and twenty-six minutes before you belong to me.

Jamie squeaked and clutched her hands so hard her knuckles scraped against each other. "Oh *my God*, I can't even with this man."

Neither could she.

* * *

After selecting several swimsuits, a couple of cocktail dresses and a few casual day outfits, Jamie had shifted his attention to her admittedly pathetic collection of lingerie.

He had summarily vetoed her few old standbys in addition to pretty much all the underwear she owned, opting to drag her to a boutique, where she'd spent nearly an entire paycheck on every silky, lacy, candy-colored confection that he'd pointed out.

Bag packed and parked by the front door, Charlotte endured the longest night of her entire life. Despite the cocktails Jamie practically poured down her throat to settle her jangling nerves, sleep eluded her completely.

She abandoned her bed by 7:00 a.m. and started coffee, surprised when her mother appeared in the doorway of the small but sunny yellow kitchen.

Rebecca Westbrook typically didn't stir until after 9:00 a.m., her night meds casting a thick blanket over her that left her groggy and sullen until Gail helped her through breakfast and a shower.

"Morning, Mom," Charlotte said, reaching into the fridge for the salted caramel–flavored Ensure her mother favored and shaking it briskly. "Ready for your drink?"

Her mother's ash-white hair stuck up in an electric shock, her pale lips frowning, her watery blue eyes squinted in a familiar expression Charlotte thought of as *searching*. Combing the vast spider web of memory to place herself in space and time.

"Gail?"

"She'll be here in just a bit," Charlotte said, opening an Ensure and sliding in a hot-pink straw. Once her mother was distracted by her drink, Charlotte fished her pill strip from its hiding place and tumbled the small handful into a medicine cup, which she set on the counter.

Her mother took them obediently, routine being the scaffold buttressing her day.

"We have to get the roses planted today, Mary."

Mary had been her mother's late baby sister, and for some reason, Charlotte had assumed her place in the world.

Shuffling over to the door leading to the small, wood-fenced backyard, Charlotte hauled back the curtains so the rosebushes were in full view, just now beginning to burst in riotous reds, ballet-slipper pinks and petticoat white.

"Aren't they beautiful?" she said, having learned long ago that attempting to directly contradict her mother's conception of reality was an exhausting lesson in futility for them both.

Her mother blinked as she took in what should be a familiar sight. "Can we go to the nursery today?"

"I'm afraid I can't take you, because I'm going to be gone for a few days, but I bet Jamie and Gail would love to go with you."

"Jamie's in Boston."

It was these casually pronounced accurate facts that made the disease that much harder to accept on a regular basis.

"That's right," Charlotte said, "but he's visiting us right now."

Her mother placed a warm palm on her cheek and

looked at Charlotte more directly than she had in half a year's time. "Be happy, Mary," she said.

Tears stung Charlotte's eyes as she placed her hand over her mother's, feeling her papery skin and spindly bones beneath.

Mary, her mother's sister, had drowned when she was sixteen.

Her mother had told her the story in detail after Charlotte had discovered a picture of them together when she was roughly the same age. Before that, she hadn't even known she'd had an aunt once upon a time.

"Coffee." Jamie appeared in the doorway in a T-shirt and rumpled boxers, his blond hair a tangled rat's nest sleep-mashed on one side.

Charlotte set out two mugs, the sugar bowl and a carton of half-and-half from the fridge. They sat together at the small kitchen table, watching their mother whisper to herself and make her circuit through the living room into the kitchen and around the dining room, only to begin again.

"We're going to be okay, I promise," Jamie assured her.

"I haven't been away from her for more than two days in three years." Guilt plucked at her, remembering Parker Kane's not-completely-disapproving reaction.

"That's exactly *why* you need to do this." Jamie lifted the steaming mug to his lips and sipped.

"You have the schedule and instructions I wrote down? And the list of emergency numbers?"

"I have all the things." He set his coffee mug aside and took her hand in his, their fingers interlocking in a laced pattern that left their pinkie fingers entwined. Their secret handshake. "Sis, I got this."

Charlotte blew out a gusty breath. "Okay, then. Let's get me ready."

Jamie drew her a lavender-scented bath that she was still soaking resplendently in when Gail arrived.

Thence followed makeup, a lengthy blowout provided by her brother and a breakfast of which Charlotte could only eat approximately three bites.

"You're going to need the energy," he had said, earning a half-eaten piece of toast lobbed at his face.

And then it was 11:50 a.m. and Jamie was at the window facing the street, peeking through the wooden slat blinds every thirty seconds.

"Get away from there," Charlotte scolded, her palms damp as she smoothed down the dress her brother had picked out for her. Body-hugging knit fabric in a hue one shade lighter than her own skin, sleeveless and brushing the top of her knees.

"Is he going to come in? He has to come in, right?" Jamie asked.

"I have no idea if—"

"Oh my God, he's here!"

Charlotte's stomach death-rolled as excitement sizzled from the tips of her fingers to her toes. She recognized the *beep-boop* of the Aston being locked from the key fob.

Dear God, he *was* coming in.

Jamie looked at her, his face a mask of openmouthed wonder.

She knew the feeling.

Are you kidding me? her brother mouthed as he saw Mason Kane for the very first time.

Heart hammering, she drew in a shaky breath as the musical chimes of the doorbell tinkled through the house. She motioned for Jamie to get away from the door, but he ignored her completely, swinging it wide to reveal a somewhat surprised Mason.

He wore an off-white dress shirt, sleeves rolled to the elbows, and jeans that fit him like sin fit the devil.

"Hi," he said in his charm-the-pants-off-anything-with-a-pulse voice, "is Charlotte—"

His words snapped off abruptly when he spotted her.

"Hi," she said, lifting her hand in what might have been the most awkward wave in the history of man. "Please, come in."

Jamie stepped back to grant him entrance, and then wonder of wonders, Mason Kane was standing in their little suburban duplex.

"This is my brother, Jamie," she said by way of introduction.

How surreal it was to see Mason shake hands with the boy she'd eaten cereal next to on Saturday mornings, bellies pressed against the cheap carpet and cartoons flickering in a Technicolor sheen over their eyes.

"Pleasure to meet you," Mason said.

"Are you the doctor?"

Her mother had chosen that exact moment to enter from the back door, a basket of roses swinging from her arm and Gail at her side.

"I could be." Mason didn't miss a beat, holding out his hand. "Mason Kane. It's a pleasure to meet you, Mrs. Westbrook."

And to Charlotte's great surprise, her mother took it, giggling like a girl when Mason lifted her hand to his lips and kissed the thin, age-spotted flesh of her knuckles.

She and Jamie snagged glances.

"Those are tea roses, right?" Mason angled his chin toward the basket. "My mother loved these, too. Said they smelled the sweetest."

The past tense of that sentence shot an arrow straight to Charlotte's heart.

Even though it had been fourteen years since Ellen Kane had passed, Charlotte had frequently encountered her name in the records for various charities and foundations that had been created in her honor. Only in the process of proofing a biography Samuel had sent her for a tribute at the Philadelphia Philharmonic's spring review had she discovered that Ellen had loved detective novels.

When she saw the names of all three Kane heirs listed together, she'd made the connection. Samuel Spade. Perry Mason. Philip Marlowe.

She had tried to imagine Parker Kane as an expectant father, allowing his twin sons and only daughter to be named after fictional characters. Charlotte could hardly reconcile that imagined man with the dour-visaged tyrant who owned her days and haunted her nights.

"Would you like one?" her mother asked in her airy, reedy voice as she offered up the basket.

"I'd love one." Mason stepped forward and plucked a small, intricately folded peaches and cream–colored bloom from the bunch and lifted it to his nose. His eyes closed as he inhaled, his smile widening.

"Lovely," he said.

Rapture melted all traces of illness from their mother's face, and for a brief moment, she was a girl again. Expectant and pleased.

"I know just where this needs to go." He treated their mother to the full, blinding wattage of his rogue's grin. "If you don't mind?"

"Not at all." A sixty-year-old coquette.

With a quick flick of his fingers, Mason snapped off a length of green stem and tucked it behind their mother's ear, standing back like a museum patron to assess. "Perfect," he said.

I. Am. Dead, Jamie mouthed behind Mason's back.

"Ready?" Mason asked.

Truly, she didn't know if she would ever be ready. Especially after the moment she'd just witnessed.

"Ready as I'll ever be." She gave Jamie a brief, fierce hug before planting a kiss on her mother's cheek.

Mason pressed the button to release the handle of her carry-on bag and rolled it toward the door.

Charlotte slung her purse over her shoulder and followed him, surprised when her mother drew her back with a firm grip on her upper arm. "Be happy, Mary."

For that one brief moment, she wasn't searching. She'd found the exact phrase she wanted for this occasion and drove it home with clear blue eyes.

"I will," Charlotte said, squeezing her mother's hand. "I promise."

Seven

Mason loaded Charlotte's carry-on bag in the Aston's trunk before swinging around to open the passenger-side door for her.

Her skin, dress and long, loose red hair were a graduation on the color scale even more delicate and beautiful than the roses in her mother's basket. In the days before he'd been shunted from the fine arts program to the far more lucrative field of marketing, at his father's behest, he would have itched to paint her.

He brushed the thought away in favor of the comfort of being in control of a fast, powerful machine.

"I really like your family," he said.

He had often felt this kind of disorientation when he was around people for whom casual displays of affection were the norm. It had seemed so effortless, the kissed cheeks and hugs passing between Charlotte and her brother.

Mason's mother had done her best, but despite her warmth, she had never quite managed to counter the chill their father cast over the house. Though she'd effortlessly doled out hugs and cuddles to her children, Mason, Samuel and Marlowe had never quite gotten the hang of how to exchange this basic social currency between them.

"They certainly liked you," Charlotte answered, her tone guarded.

"Your mother—" he began.

"Alzheimer's," she said, confirming precisely what he'd suspected.

"How long?" he asked, angling his torso to face her.

"She was diagnosed three years ago, but she's taken a sharp turn."

"I'm very sorry."

"Well, we can both be sorry." She shifted in her seat, nervously tugging at the edge of her skirt in a way that made Mason want to drag it up to her hips. "I lied to your father."

"With all due respect, I've been lying to my father since I acquired language." He set a hand on her bare knee, the contact making his palm tingle. "There is nothing you could have said that will surpass the many and various fictions he's endured from me."

"I told him that the reason I needed the week off is because my brother came to town for a surprise visit." Her eyes were cast down at her lap in remorse.

"But your brother *is* in town for a surprise visit," he

said, amused to see a small wedge of shadow present between two of the blind slats facing the street.

"But that's not *why* I'm taking the time off," she pointed out.

A quiet thrill shot through him, *I Can Justify Anything* being one of his all-time favorite games.

"Let's think about this," he said, leaning back in his seat. "If your brother weren't in town, it would have been damn near impossible for you to go on this trip. Correct?"

"Correct." She nodded.

"And did you tell my father that the reason you were taking the time off was specifically to spend it with your brother?"

"Not specifically," she admitted.

"Boom," he said. "No lies detected."

She let out a sigh and rolled her eyes at him. "I feel like you and the truth are in an open relationship."

"As opposed to a codependent relationship with guilt?" he suggested.

By the look on her face, he guessed he might have aimed a little too close to the mark.

"All I mean is," he quickly recovered, "you strike me as someone who has a difficult time letting herself off the hook. And if approval from an authority outside yourself is required to do so, then think of me as your permission slip."

Her downy cheek dimpled as she chewed the inside, a nervous habit he'd noticed on more than one occasion.

Mason glanced back toward the duplex. "Either way, we should be on our way before your brother has a coronary."

"On this point, I agree entirely." She crossed one leg over the other, the hem of her dress creeping up her thigh. "When are we wheels up?"

Wheels up.

How many times had she used this precise term in emails to the executive team without ever having been on the flight in question?

"We're wheels up when I tell them they're up." He started the Aston's engine and pulled away from the curb. "We have a stop to make first."

"Where?" Charlotte asked, eyes keen with interest.

"You'll see."

Half an hour later, he eased the car up to the curb front of Retrospect, a boutique in an unassuming red-brick building in Philadelphia's trendy Fishkill neighborhood.

The afternoon sun wove glowing red-gold threads into Charlotte's hair as she examined the storefront. "What's this?"

"A present." He found himself in the precarious position of not wanting to ask her what she'd packed and wanting her to pick out something she hadn't packed but would never buy for herself.

"In addition to an all-expenses-paid vacation to the French Riviera?" she asked, opening her door before he had a chance.

South Street was quiet on a Saturday afternoon, the brunch crowd having dispersed elsewhere in Society Hill.

An automated chime tolled when they entered the building, and the proprietress looked up from behind

a staggeringly large arrangement of freesia in the entryway.

"Well, if it isn't Little Lord Kane."

Kassidy Nichols was the kind of woman he had strenuously avoided in his adult life. Namely, because the
lazy-river float of his sexual exploits generally proved
unacceptable to someone of her relentless intelligence,
unfailing ambition and unblinkingly analytical mind.

Charlotte tensed at his side. "You know each other?"

Biblically? was the subtext of the question, and he
felt an instant and unfamiliar need to reassure her.

"Kassidy was the valedictorian of our class at Len-
nox Finch. She's also Arlie's best friend."

"If you know Arlie, then you're already family," Kassidy said, looking at Charlotte with infinite warmth.
"What brings you in today?"

"We need at least two formal dresses," Mason answered.

"Formal as in Met Gala or formal as in standard
black-tie affair?" she asked.

"*Euro* black tie."

A knowing smile creased Kassidy's lips. "Wait here."

She returned with a rolling rack of hanging gowns
in deep forest greens, pale lavenders and blush pinks.

He could feel Charlotte's sharp intake of breath as
she took them in.

"Go ahead," Mason urged.

She stepped forward, her fingers sliding over the fabric of one dress after the other with a sensuousness that
filled him with an irrational surge of jealousy.

"These are lovely," she said.

Kassidy raised an eyebrow at him the second Charlotte looked away. "Thank you."

He shrugged and aimed a roguish grin that earned him a roll of her amber eyes.

"Are there any you'd like to try on?" Kassidy asked.

"All of them?" Charlotte's laugh was as carefree and accidental as the ringing of a crystal bell, and Mason felt himself stunned to the very core when he realized this was the first time he'd ever heard it.

"Let me get you set up in a room here." Kassidy wheeled the rack over to a row of brocade curtains and parted them, revealing a small but lush stall with mirrors on three sides. She lifted the first dress and hung it on a polished silver hook, waiting until Charlotte was inside to pull the curtains closed.

"And what, may I ask, are you doing?" she asked in a harsh, hushed whisper when she had returned to Mason.

"Supporting local business?"

"The charming-wastrel bullshit isn't going to fly with me, Kane." Kassidy crossed her arms over a generous bosom that he found himself not the least bit tempted to imagine beneath the silky fabric of her beautifully cut blouse, for perhaps the first time in his entire life. "That girl in there is three parts Cinderella and one part Bambi. Now, I know you stepped in to help Arlie when the shit hit the fan with her and Samuel, and I appreciate it, but we both know that doesn't make you Prince Charming."

The accusation stung. In no small part because he couldn't argue the truthfulness of her statement. Or deny that it slithered into his consciousness many times since she had agreed to come with him.

Just then, the curtains parted, and Charlotte's head poked through, a shy smile on her face. "A little help?"

"Be right there," Kassidy called before turning to him with a beseeching expression softening her features. "Think about it, is all I'm saying."

With that, she marched off to help.

He stood at the counter, his thoughts a hectic tangle as, one by one, the dresses disappeared behind the curtain and reappeared on the rack.

At last, Kassidy emerged with a black garment bag that she set on the counter before turning her attention to the iPad register, tapping in numbers.

Charlotte joined him a couple minutes later, her hair slightly fuzzed, her eyes bugging when she glanced at the number on the register screen.

Kassidy leveled him with an I-told-you-so stare.

Mason reached into his wallet and plugged his card into the slot, removing it when prompted.

"Email or paper receipt?" Kassidy asked, plum-colored lips pursed.

"Neither," he said, lifting the garment bag from the counter. "Thank you."

"Enjoy," she said, giving him a pointed look.

Back in the car, Charlotte glanced back at the garment bag as they pulled away from the curb. "You really didn't need to do that."

"I wanted to." Only now, having been flayed by the scalpel of Kassidy's observations, he found himself wondering *why*. If his motives were as pure as he'd initially thought.

Brushing away the involuntary introspection, he

stepped hard enough on the accelerator to make Charlotte squeak in surprise.

"Buckle up," he said, though she clearly already had. "We've got a jet to catch."

And catch it they did.

Charlotte's mouth dropped open as they neared the sleek, angular Falcon 7X private jet waiting for them on the tarmac.

"It's not one of the Kane Foods fleet, I'm sorry to say." Mason angled a sideways grin at her. "But under the circumstances, I thought it best."

The shuttle driver who had conveyed them from valet parking to the designated airfield parked near the Falcon's extended staircase and got out of the car, coming around to open Charlotte's door.

She exited and stood staring while their driver transferred the luggage to the uniformed attendant, who loaded it into the jet's cargo area in turn.

"Ready?" Mason asked, sliding a hand around her hips.

"Absolutely not," she said when she had recovered her composure. "Lead the way."

"Good afternoon, Mr. Kane." A flight attendant in a cream-colored blouse and pleated navy skirt greeted them with a polite nod. "My name is Amanda, and I'll be taking care of you both this afternoon. Please make yourselves comfortable, and don't hesitate to let me know if you need anything at all."

"Thank you, Amanda," Mason said, quickly moving out of the way and positioning himself so he could see Charlotte's face as she took in the cabin for the first time.

The pure, unvarnished wonder of her expression alone was worth the sixty thousand it had cost him to charter the flight. Her brown eyes were wide behind the black frames of her glasses, her eyebrows lifted toward her hairline, her mouth a perfect oval.

She strolled forward, trailing a hand across the buttery cream-colored leather sofa in the lounge area. The small table beside it bore a sweating silver bucket of ice, a bottle of Moët & Chandon Esprit du Siècle Brut planted in it like a spring tulip. Across from this, two sets of generous leather seats of the same hue faced each other across a gleaming table of polished walnut.

Charlotte put her shoulder bag down on it and dug out a small notebook. "You don't mind if I—" She motioned around the cabin.

"I'd be disappointed if you didn't." Mason seated himself on the couch, contentedly observing as she buzzed from point to point like a hummingbird, scribbling notes, presumably for her novel.

Amanda returned with two slim champagne flutes and set them near the bucket, a question in her eyes. *Did Mason want her to pour?*

He shook his head no, rising to peel the gilded foil and unspool the metal wire holding the fat cork in place. It shot out with a familiar *pop*, billowing with foam that Mason slurped before filling their glasses.

"To a week in paradise," he said, lifting his.

Charlotte's smile was endearingly shy. "A week in paradise."

They clinked and drank; the champagne was dry and sharp on his tongue.

"Pardon my intrusion." Amanda stood at a respectful distance, her limbs arranged in an expertly deferential posture. "We've received approval for takeoff. I'm afraid we'll need you both seated and buckled in until we reach cruising altitude."

"Of course," Mason said, then turned to Charlotte. "Where will it be?"

She collected her shoulder bag before strolling toward the front of the cabin, where a floor-to-ceiling privacy screen separated two forward-facing chairs from the rest of the craft.

"Is this okay?" she asked, settling into the one nearest the window.

"Perfect." He seated himself next to her and was completely, utterly shocked when Charlotte reached across his lap, fishing beside his hip to find his seat belt and drag it slowly and *very* deliberately over his crotch.

"Is *this* okay?" She looked at him from beneath the dark fringe of her lowered lashes.

He was so caught off guard by her boldness that he altogether failed to answer her. Or maybe he was tongue-tied because of the burgeoning fire deep in his gut signaling blood was about to be diverted from his brain to regions farther south.

She aimed an innocent smile at him as she found the other side and clicked it in, tugging on the black strap to fasten it.

His mouth having gone suddenly dry, Mason reached for his champagne and sipped it, relishing the cold, citrusy bite.

Charlotte sat back in her seat and reached for her own glass before turning her face to the jet's oblong window. Soft light highlighted the curve of her jaw, scattering threads of copper like a halo around the hair she'd worn long and loose.

Amanda appeared again, informing them apologetically that she would need to collect their glasses for takeoff but would bring them back once they'd reached altitude.

Mason drained the last of his and handed it over, secretly pleased when Charlotte did the same.

She had an appetite after all.

One he suspected had never been properly acknowledged or satiated. A situation that he intended to rectify in short order.

"Enjoy your flight," Amanda said, giving them a starched smile before bustling off toward the other end of the cabin.

As soon as she was gone, Mason shifted to make visible the area of his crotch he'd hidden with a conveniently placed forearm.

Charlotte's mouth dropped open a fraction as the wet, pink tip of her tongue slid over her pillowy lower lip. He would have sworn he could *feel* the leisurely caress of her regard as it moved down his length before rising to meet his.

"Tell me something," he said.

"Yes?" Her eyelashes fluttered, all signs of the temptress having utterly vanished.

"Do you like getting me hard?" He heard the rasp in his own voice and knew she'd caught it, too.

Roses spilled into her cheeks, and she quickly looked away. "Why do you ask?"

"It's like you only feel comfortable letting that side of yourself out when it's less likely that anything can happen as a result."

The corner of her mouth tugged downward in a frown.

"If it makes you feel powerful, and that's all you want to feel, I'm a big boy and I can take it. But if it's because you're afraid—" he paused, waiting for her to look at him "—then I need to understand why. If it's me you're afraid of—"

"It's not," she broke in.

Gently, he reached across the lowered leather armrest separating their seats and took her hand in his. "Then what?"

When she turned, the answer was written all over her face. "I haven't really dated much. I was with the same person for most of college and, I don't know. I just struggle with being…adventurous." Her laugh was small and self-effacing. "He said I saved all my best material for the page."

"He told you that?" he demanded, his anger rising. She looked away from him.

"First," he said, irritation at her ex oily in his stomach, "this guy is clearly an asshole and had no idea who you are and what he had. Second, never, ever compare yourself to anyone from my past and assume you're the one who's lacking. Got it?"

She gave him a hesitant nod.

"Finally, you need understand that the reason I'm sitting here hard as a fucking diamond is because just breathing the same air as you is making me crazy."

Their gazes locked in the wake of that admission and held as the jet began to roll forward, the tarmac and patches of green beyond like a moving tapestry in the window behind her.

Something passed between them in that second.

"How long from takeoff until we reach altitude?" she asked, cutting her eyes back toward the crew area.

"In a jet this size? About ten minutes."

With a dreamy haze in her eyes, Charlotte reached beneath his seat belt and found the brass flag of his zipper, slowly sliding it down. One flick and her fingers slipped inside, navigating to the fly of his boxer briefs to find the hot, pulsing skin beneath.

He sucked in a hissing breath, marveling at the sensation that shot from her questing hand to his soul by way of his cock.

The plane began to pick up speed, and Charlotte leaned as far over as her seat belt would allow, her hair falling across his lap like a curtain. She freed him from his pants, the sight of her delicate fingers wrapped around him releasing a tidal wave of need.

Her breath was warm on his turgid flesh, and he gasped when she closed her mouth over him just as the jet lifted off from the gray blur of the runway.

The combination of that stomach-flipping ascension in tandem with his sinking into the hot, wet socket of her mouth had Mason gripping the armrest, his knuckles white. His low, quiet moan was absorbed into the jet engine's roar, but Charlotte's vibrated from her lips to his fevered skin.

There was a wildness in the way that she took him. In the eager, unstudied earnestness with which she pursued his pleasure. And after so long without, the intensity of the sensations she produced threatened to rocket him straight over the edge.

Mason gathered her glorious hair in a glossy skein at the base of her neck and gently tugged it to slow her progression.

"That's it," he coaxed, timing his breaths to her motion, concentrating on maintaining his quickly unraveling control. "Just like that."

As if sensing his effort to slow their pace, she began moving her fist with liquid smoothness in concert with her mouth, pausing to circle his throbbing head with silky swirls of her tongue.

"Oh, God," Mason panted under his breath.

This was exquisite torture. Him, fastened into a seat, unable to move with her, surrendering to his undoing.

Charlotte lifted her head to look up at him, the hunger in those wide molten-chocolate eyes setting an answering blaze in his soul.

Because he understood that she wanted to see his face. To watch exactly what she was doing to him. To feel the power she wielded over him.

He was sinking and rising and melting into the swirling heat in his center. That great, coiled energetic serpent crackling with the frustration of these lonely months—years, maybe—seeking release. Seeking oblivion.

Just when he was on the precipice, nearly ready to tumble into that dark, decadent release, he stopped her. His fingers tightening ever so slightly in her hair, his hand fastened over hers to arrest the motion.

"Not yet," he ground out.

Charlotte carefully lifted her head, concern crumpling her brow as she released him and sat up.

Mason pushed her hair back from her face, smoothing away the lines worry had etched there.

"Not before we get there," he murmured, blood still rioting within him. "I want to be inside you when I come."

A smile curved her lips, now half denuded of lipstick. She pulled a tissue from a pack in her shoulder bag and dabbed her lips before offering it to him.

Mason took it and quickly cleaned himself up, pocketing the evidence and collapsing back against his seat. When he had recovered his breath, he rolled his head on the headrest to face her.

"PS," he whispered, leaning closer, running his thumb over her lower lip before pulling her in for a kiss that tasted of salt and sex and the ghost of champagne. "Your ex is a fucking moron."

A musical *ping* preceded their captain announcing they had reached cruising altitude.

"Shall we roam?" Mason asked, unbuckling his seat belt.

They settled themselves onto the leather couch in the sitting area.

Shortly thereafter, Amanda reappeared, and Mason couldn't help but grin inwardly as Charlotte quickly scanned her face. Searching, no doubt, for any clue that might indicate they'd been busted.

"Can I bring you more champagne, or would you like something else to drink?" Amanda asked, conveying not a jot of suspicion or disapproval.

Charlotte visibly relaxed in his peripheral vision. "Bourbon," she said. "With a rock."

"I'll have the same," he said.

"Not scotch?" Charlotte asked curiously when Amanda had gone.

Mason placed his hand on her knee, his fingers flexing against her bare inner thigh. "Bourbon tastes like you."

Amanda brought their drinks, and they sat sipping in companionable silence.

The bourbon was cool and smoky but did little to banish the bitterness of his thoughts. To imagine some mediocre jackass lucky enough to be in bed with Charlotte Westbrook, chipping away at her self-confidence with careless blows.

That shit would be changing, effective immediately, even if he accomplished nothing else this week.

Ten hours, one fuel stop and mountains of sexual tension later, they were making their final descent into the Nice Côte d'Azur Airport.

Charlotte leaned against the window, her face painted in childlike excitement as she peered down at the ludicrously blue waters of the Ligurian Sea.

"So beautiful," she whispered, softly touching her own cheek.

Yes, you are was all Mason could think.

They bumped down on the runway and both switched their phones off airplane mode to an outraged combined chorus of pings and beeps.

Mason glanced at his screen and felt the first stirrings of alarm when he saw Marlowe's name and a long series of texts beginning with where the hell are you? and ending with if you're doing what I think you're doing you must have lost what remained of your mind. CALL. ME.

He had been so distracted trying to quickly assemble a plausible lie that he had utterly failed to notice the shock etched into Charlotte's face.

Eight

Why aren't you at home?

Charlotte reread the words until they became strange, angry, meaningless glyphs on the glowing screen of her phone.

Another number she didn't recognize.

Whoever sent the message knew.

Knew she'd blocked the number the previous message had come from. Knew she wasn't at home, and now, apparently, knew where home was.

Or did they?

Was this some kind of sick attempt to scare her? A thoughtless prank?

"What is it?" Mason asked, clearly seeing her alarm.

She quickly darkened the phone screen and placed it facedown in her lap. "Just an email I forgot about.

I'll take care of it when we get to the—" She paused. "Where are we staying again?"

His eyes narrowed. For someone she had previously thought to be generally oblivious to anything that didn't hold immediate interest for him, he was proving to be far more observant and shrewd than she'd realized.

It wasn't that Charlotte felt any compelling need to keep the texts from him. Just that she wasn't sure that involving him when she didn't even know what was actually going on made any sense.

Thankfully, he decided to let it go.

"Château du Ciel villa, near St. Tropez. It's about a forty-minute drive from here."

When they were properly docked and disembarked, Charlotte tapped out a quick note to Jamie while their luggage was transferred to a sleek black Lamborghini. She hadn't expected a reply as her brother was famous for putting his phone on Do Not Disturb every night, so was surprised when his response was immediate.

Glad you made it safe! Mom is fine. I'm fine. Everyone's fine. Go misbehave.

Charlotte smiled, hesitating before sending her next message. Will do. Just out of curiosity, has anyone stopped by for me?

She held her breath, relieved to see a simple Nope?? in reply.

Okay. Get back to sleep. Love you, James, she quickly fired back.

Once saddled up in the car, Mason turned to her as

the Lamborghini purred away from the airport. "I hope you don't object to our taking the scenic route."

She reached into the shoulder bag at her feet and withdrew her notebook and pen, jotting down words and images as they flashed into her head, desperate to capture everything.

"You could always take pictures," he suggested. "For later analysis."

"Pictures I can get on the internet," Charlotte said. "And I do, when that's all I can get. But *being* there— that's a whole other thing."

"I guess I could see that," he said.

She wondered if this was actually true.

Mason expertly geared the engine down as they zipped around a curve. "Look," he said.

Breath escaped her in a whooshing "wow" as she peered through the windshield. The winding road had opened up on a panoramic view of endless blue dotted with a scattering of boats. Sailboats, speedboats and slips. Long, gleaming, multistoried yachts that put Parker Kane's *Dolce Vita* to shame.

Above that limpid azure expanse, a rocky outcropping gave way to a green slope with clusters of old brick buildings with terra-cotta roofs, the elegant fingers of cypress trees tickling the cloud-streaked sky.

She returned her attention to her notebook, leaving Mason to stay lost in thoughts that kept him unusually silent.

About a half an hour had passed when he slowed as they made a sharp turn off the main road.

"Home stretch," he announced.

As they climbed the hillside, she felt the kind of

bubbling excitement that had always kept her eyes frozen wide in the long hours between Christmas Eve and Christmas morning, her palms damp with anticipation.

Then the tree line broke, and a wrought-iron gate barred the path ahead. Mason pulled up to a rectangular call box and pressed a button.

"May I help you?" The voice was polite, and Charlotte could hear a posh English accent despite the intercom's slight crackle.

"Mason Kane," he said, as if this were the answer to every potential question.

The panel beeped, and the gate parted and swung inward.

A sprawling three-story Italianate villa appeared like a mirage, growing larger as they approached. Ivy-lined and flanked by more cypress trees, its many windows were smeared blue with the reflected sky.

They pulled into the circular drive and stopped before the massive double doors of inlaid wood and were promptly greeted by a silver-haired man in a neat tweed suit who rushed to help Charlotte out of the car.

Somewhere, a fountain cheerfully burbled, punctured by the distant cry of seagulls and the sigh of wind through the surrounding trees. No engines rumbling or sirens screaming. No bustling hum of humans crowded together in the city.

Drawing her first breath of this quiet, she felt an actual, physical release somewhere deep within her.

"Welcome to Château du Ciel, Miss Westbrook," the silver-haired man said with a quick, deferential nod. "My name is Hobson, and I'll be keeping an eye on things while you're in residence. Should you need any-thing at all, please don't hesitate to ask."

Hobson motioned to a porter, who jogged down from the broad stone steps to collect their bags.

"If you could have them brought to the balcony suite, Hobson." Mason held out a neat fold of bills to him.

"Of course," he said, accepting the tip with a flour-ish. "Pleasure to see you again, Mr. Kane."

Again.

The word curdled in her stomach.

He had been here before. And with whom?

She pushed the thought away, reminding herself once again that her focus was here, now. To soak in every possible detail. To fill the creative well bled bone-dry from years of routine and worry.

"Charlotte?"

Mason stood on the bottom stair, his green eyes bright, his hand held out to her.

His palm was rough and warm, his fingers strong as they closed over her knuckles. An electric jolt shot all the way to her elbow, a delicate flutter waking in her middle at this seemingly casual but intimate gesture.

Another young man with a crisp uniform and flaw-less olive complexion opened the door as they ap-proached. It was wide enough for them to walk through side by side, and when they had, Charlotte found herself stopping dead in her tracks.

She hadn't realized her mouth had dropped open until Mason gently closed it for her with a gentle tap of his index finger beneath her chin.

They stood in a soaring entryway, a grand marble staircase on their right and a vast, lushly appointed living space with a giant fireplace on their left. And straight ahead, three-story floor-to-ceiling windows overlooked the sea beyond a stone courtyard. At one end, an infinity pool stretched into the horizon, its sides dotted with plush lounge chairs and several cabanas, their filmy curtains fluttering.

"Want to take a look?" he asked.

She nodded, having lost the ability to speak.

They walked together across the entryway, turning down a side hallway to a set of glass doors that opened onto the courtyard. From this vantage, she could see an ornate, sculptural fountain at the center and the border of orange trees growing from giant planters.

Unable to resist, she stepped out of her heels and walked along the eternity pool to the edge of the terrace, the slate beneath her bare feet warmed by the morning sun. A breeze gusted up from the steep drop-off of the overlook, lifting her hair from her neck and playing with the floating edge of her skirt.

He was behind her.

His broad, muscular chest pressed against her shoulder blades. He wrapped his arms around her, one forearm resting above her breasts, the other banded across her belly. Awareness came alive in her body as she felt the warmth of his skin through her clothes. There was the barest scrape of stubble against her jaw as he brought his mouth near her ear.

"Beautiful, isn't it?"

"There are no words," she whispered.

"Isn't having words the entire point?" he asked, a teasing note in his voice. He nuzzled the base of her neck, releasing a flood of gooseflesh down her bare arms.

"Is it?" she asked.

She felt his abdominal muscles tense against her lower back. This wasn't the kind of question she had meant to ask him. But standing like this, she had to wonder if he had been so casually affectionate with all the women in his retinue.

And if so, how they could feel safe in the circle of his arms and not want to stay there forever? How could they occupy that space while knowing that others did, and had, and would?

"What was that?" he asked.

"Nothing." She chickened out, pulling away from him and attempting a smile. "Show me around?"

His smile faltered, but he nodded, taking her hand once again. "I'll give you the grand tour."

Grand it was.

Every sweeping corridor, soaring ceiling and dazzling view.

After Mason had squired her through nearly every corner with contagious, if exhausting, enthusiasm, they paused at the end of the hallway on the third floor.

"This—" he pushed down on the ornate brass handle and nudged the door open "—is your suite."

A giant, ornately carved four-poster canopy bed faced a wide bank of windows, curtains billowing like sails in the breeze from doors open to a balcony overlooking both the pool and the sea beyond.

She wandered past the end of the bed and into a bathroom that was about half as large as the house she shared with her mother. There was floor-to-ceiling marble, a deep oversize jetted tub and separate glass-enclosed shower with a complicated series of knobs and nozzles that Charlotte had exactly no confidence that she'd be able to work.

Yet, despite the overwhelmingly lovely surroundings, she couldn't help but feel a small stab of disappointment.

Her suite.

Naive of her, she supposed, to assume they would be staying in the same room. That he wouldn't want his own space.

The phone in the front pocket of Mason's shirt buzzed, and pulled it out, glanced down at the screen, frowned and silenced it.

"Well," he said, "I'll give you a few hours to refresh yourself and settle in. Meet me in the foyer at two?"

Something inside her wilted at the businesslike manner in which he suggested this. Why had she been so certain he would take her on the first available surface the second they arrived?

Crestfallen but hoping not to show it, she gave him a neutral smile. "If I can find it."

He pecked a quick kiss on her cheek and left.

After waiting a few beats,, she cracked open the door he'd closed behind him. At the end of the hall, Mason took his phone out of his pocket and held it to his cheek.

Had this palatial residence less impressive acoustics, she wouldn't have heard the first three words he spoke as he descended the stairs.

"How's my girl?"

She stood there in her travel-rumpled clothes, her face stinging like she'd just been slapped.

My girl?

Who, exactly, had she been kidding? Believing that

Mason Kane, legendary billionaire womanizer of the Philadelphia elite, was going to just flip a switch and devote his attention entirely to her. Even for the brief span of seven days? And assuming she actually believed he'd ceased physical contact with his former flings, did that guarantee he wasn't still talking with any of them?

Fuming, she crossed to the bench where the porter had set out her carry-on bag and began digging through it, shoving her clothes in the drawers of the dresser and roughly hanging the various items in the armoire. The garment bag bearing the dresses Mason had purchased for her at Retrospect had already been neatly hung.

This whole exercise killed approximately fifteen minutes.

She considered taking a bath, but the thought of sitting still in steaming water made her skin feel itchy and hot.

Returning to the dresser, she located the emerald-green halter bikini Jamie had insisted she bring, along with the matching cover-up, and quickly changed into them. In front of the full-length cheval mirror, she hastily braided her hair before grabbing a book and her phone from her purse and setting off in the general direction of the main staircase.

Her walk to the pool proved blessedly uninterrupted. Once there, she picked up a fluffy towel from the cabinet near the door and spread it out over one of the reclining loungers. After a glance around to confirm she was alone, she undid the belt of her cover-up and draped it over the lounger.

Under normal circumstances, she would have slicked her pale, freckled skin with SPF 100, but it was early enough in the day and she planned on being here no longer than it would take to power through enough laps to clear her head.

Though she hadn't made a regular habit of swimming as her primary form of exercise since college, she could reliably exert herself to pure, sweet exhaustion relatively quickly.

The tiles at the bottom of the pool were a cobalt blue, the water just cool enough to be refreshing as it lapped at her calves, her thighs, her waist. She sank to her neck, then plunged under the surface, pushing off hard against the wall.

She dolphin kicked beneath the water until she needed to come up for air, quickly falling into the familiar pattern of kicks and strokes her coach had programmed into her body.

And in that kingdom between water and sky, it all fell away. Her jealousy. Her guilt. Her fear. The opposite wall of the pool brushed her fingertips, and she somersaulted, exhilaration surging through her as she sliced through the water, faster than her thoughts.

Until something caught her ankle.

Nine

Charlotte shrieked and nearly took in a lungful of water, coughing and sputtering, wiping her eyes as Mason's apologies rained down on her.

He began taking shape in her blurred, blinking vision, his chest bare and water-speckled, hands on her upper arms steadying her.

"Shit, are you okay?"

Dragging in a labored breath, she brought her hands to her thundering heart. "What the hell? Why would you do that?"

"I'm—I'm sorry, I just, saw you swimming and thought I would join you and—"

"So sit in the shallow end and *wait*." Pulling away from him, she swam to the side of the pool, anchoring her forearms over the edge while her breath slowed.

He swam up beside her and lifted the wet braid off

her neck, his hand warm between her shoulder blades. From this vantage, she saw that Mason had laid a towel on the lounger next to hers. An icy bucket of champagne, a carafe of orange juice and a basket of croissants sat on the table between them.

"I brought us refreshments," he said, apparently catching the direction of her gaze. "Does that count as an apology?"

Charlotte bobbed next to him, turning to look him in the eye. The water darkened his tawny hair, his long lashes in wet clumps around sparkling eyes made aqua by the reflection of the cobalt-blue tiles. Beads of moisture gathered on his lips and cheeks, in the corners of his uneven grin. She saw in a flash what he must have looked like as a boy and felt suddenly, irrationally protective of someone who most certainly didn't need it.

"What are you doing down here, anyway?" she asked. "I thought you had a couple hours' worth of work to do."

"I do," he said. "But how the hell am I supposed to concentrate when you're down here looking like this?" Below the water's surface, he traced the small of her back just below the waistband of her bikini bottoms, and Charlotte felt her already hardened nipples tighten against her top.

She kicked her legs lazily, her toes barely scraping the bottom of the pool.

"I'm sure mine is hardly the most scandalous attire this water has seen." She slid him a sideways glance.

Then she felt herself pulled backward. Her slippery fingers failed to find purchase on the edge of the pool as Mason dragged her into water too deep for her feet to find the bottom, and she had no choice but to cling to his smooth, warm neck as he walked her backward.

Catching her behind the knees, he wrapped her legs around his waist, his lean hipbones pressing into her inner thighs.

Hands supporting her, he pulled her against him, already hard through the thin fabric of his swim trunks.

"Why is it so difficult for you to believe it's just you I'm thinking about?" he asked.

Experience.

The word was wet ash clinging to her tongue. Coward that she was, she couldn't make herself say it. Any more than she could admit she'd spied on him after he'd left her room.

"I don't know," she said, aware it was another lame cop-out.

"What can I do to reassure you?" he asked.

Over his tattooed shoulder, she watched the yachts lazily drift across the choppy surface of the sea, sailboats zipping and darting around them.

"I don't know that, either." This, at least, was the truth. She had so little basis for comparison. She'd given herself so easily and learned so disastrously what didn't work for her, but she knew so little of what did.

"Look at me," he said.

Her stomach knotted as she clung to him. Breasts pressed against the flat planes of his chest, the water as deliciously cool as he was warm, the scent of his skin and shampoo mingled with the wind.

Pulling her attention away from the hillside dotted with old stone villas and their rust-colored terra-cotta roofs, she forced herself to meet his terribly earnest gaze.

"Kiss me, Charlotte."

All she wanted to do in that moment was turn away. To bury her face in his neck or lay her cheek on his shoulder. Anything to break the crackling, unbearable intensity of enduring his direct regard.

She wanted this as much as she wanted to feel his mouth on hers. Wanted him to drive all suspicion from her head. But he would not give her this.

He wanted her to take it.

Their breaths came faster now, his soft exhales cooling the droplets clinging to her cheeks.

Her grip on the back of his neck tightened as she leaned in close enough to feel the heat of his mouth. Hesitantly, she brushed her lips across his once. Twice. Three times. Feeling the shape of them, their contradictory smoothness and firmness. With the very tip of her tongue, she tested the seam where they met, tasting salt and pool water and the pure, chemical loveliness of him.

"You're killing me, woman." Mason's fingers tightened on her as he pressed his steely heat between her split thighs.

Galvanized by his apparent need, she deepened the kiss, sliding her tongue beneath his pliant lips, grinding against him brazenly. Delicious friction built where their bodies met, and at last, he kissed her back, his tongue tangling with hers, their teeth grazing as they devoured each other.

Her spine met with the side of the pool and, still unable to touch bottom, she slipped her arms beneath his, forearms behind the winged muscles of his back, fingers cupping his shoulders as she used the traction to glide up and down his length.

Mason's growl vibrated within their fused mouths, and his hands were everywhere. Pushing the cups of her top aside so the hard pearls of her nipples dug against his naked chest. Dragging the crotch of her bottoms aside so his fingers could explore folds slippery with water and desire.

Following suit, she reached beneath the waistband of his trunks to take his hot, velvety cock in her hand.

He made a strangled sound and pulled his mouth away from hers. His words were ragged and low in her ear. "Not here."

Mason rearranged his swimsuit and quickly helped her do the same before hauling himself up over the side of the pool and reaching a hand down to her. She took it, surprised as he lifted her from the water and onto her feet on the deck before marching her to the cabana and drawing the breezy curtains.

If she had expected him to proceed with the same urgency he'd demonstrated in the pool, she was sorely mistaken. Mason gently eased her down onto the lounge bed before lying down beside her.

With the arrogance of a man who owned the entire world and all the time in it, he slowly untied the strings of her bikini top.

Using the wet end of her braid like a brush, he painted first one nipple then the other, working in lazy circles. Charlotte squirmed at the maddening, tickling feeling, each silky flick further stoking the thickening heat at her core.

Just when she thought she would die from the teasing, he moved his mouth over one nipple while continuing to paint the other. Decadent heat on one side, puckering coolness on the other, and a riot of sensation between.

She gripped his shoulder, barely even conscious of the way her hips writhed and bucked. Needing him. Needing him so badly she wanted to cry.

"Please," she whispered.

Mason lifted his head, his eyes burning into hers. "Please *what*?"

Even scorched with desire, she couldn't force the words from her mouth.

As if in answer to her thoughts, he rose and stood facing her at the end of the lounger, hooking his fingers into the bottom of her swimsuit and dragging it down her legs.

The perfection of his powerful torso shamed the classical Greek statues littering the courtyard. He was a living, breathing masterpiece with eyes like the ocean during a squall.

He contemplated her with a faraway expression as he trailed his fingertips from the hollow at the base of her neck down to her belly button.

Her navel twitched and shuddered, her entire body drawn tight as a bowstring beneath his touch.

"So beautiful," he whispered, repeating the motion, each time venturing incrementally closer to the aching apex of her thighs.

She reached for him, eager fingers pulling at his trunks, desperate to have him.

"Not yet," he said, gently placing her hand back on her own thigh. "I need you wet."

Lifting her head, Charlotte couldn't keep the frustration from her voice. "We just got out of the pool."

Mason skimmed his swim shorts down his hips and stepped out of them.

"I need you wet *for me*," he said.

And she saw why.

What she'd felt that night in the darkened penthouse bedroom and even tasted while he was fully clothed looked completely, staggeringly different viewed in the context of his hulking naked form.

Her eyes widened as a small filament of alarm vibrated through her.

She suddenly felt silly and self-conscious, pretending she was in any way prepared for the reality of the man before her.

The soles of her feet pressed against the mattress, her legs reflexively drawn halfway to her torso. With his hands around her ankles, and a wicked grin on his lips, he rolled her flat onto her back and set them hip-width apart.

"Open your knees," he commanded.

Hesitantly, she complied.

"Wider," he said. "I want to see you."

She dared a few more inches, only to be rewarded with Mason swiftly pulling her nearly to the end of the lounger. There, he slid his forearms under her thighs and planted his hands on either side of her hips until her knees were outside his shoulders.

"When I say *wider*, this is what I mean. Understand?" A single droplet fell from his hair and landed on her cheek.

She nodded, her heart pounding so hard she could feel it in her eyelids.

Mason knelt before her, a look of such scorching

focus on his face that she fought the urge to scramble all the way to the back of the cabana.

Hands that had been on either side of her hips now flattened against her stomach, his thumbs and index fingers making a diamond around her belly button, holding her hips still.

His hot, wet tongue split her with a long, hungry lick that wrung a gasp from her.

"Such a sensitive little thing." He circled the fiery bundle of nerves, interrupting each languid circuit with occasional flicks of his tongue.

Her stomach fluttered beneath his hands.

"Mmm," he hummed against her, further intensifying the effect. "God, I love the way you taste." Rolling her bud beneath the flat of his tongue, Mason kept one hand fastened over her stomach and dragged the other over her hip, up the outside of her thigh and down the inside, gently plying her apart.

Charlotte moaned, her lower back arching, opening herself farther to him.

Mason slipped his index and middle fingers inside her, hands and mouth working in concert. Her legs began to shake, her fingers clutching at the mattress as she felt her climax rushing toward her.

"Mason." It was half cry, half warning. She fisted both hands in his hair and let loose a single soaring note of ecstasy as the pulses of pleasure gripped her until her body went entirely slack.

Rising like a god from the sea, he stood over her, his long, thick sex branding her inner thigh.

He wordlessly reached into a drawer of the table

beside the lounger, withdrew a foil packet and tore it with his perfect white teeth, quickly sheathing himself.

Mason lifted her hips and locked his eyes on hers before sliding his arousal into her with a fluid surge.

Charlotte sucked in a breath, and he stilled inside her, his expression somewhere between pleasure and pain. Worry and wonder.

"I didn't...did I...hurt you?" Damp hair fell in his eyes. His deep chest rose and fell in labored breaths.

She shook her head quickly, knowing this was not entirely true. *Hurt* wasn't the word for it. He filled her in ways she hadn't known she could be filled. Touched her in places she hadn't known existed until he reached them. He was wonderfully, terribly, perfectly beyond anything she'd ever experienced.

As if sensing her half-truth, he advanced slowly, withdrawing himself and curling back into her with a gentle, undulating roll that began in his shoulders and ended at the base of his spine. His face was a mask of concentration, his muscles taut with the effort of self-control.

By slow degrees, she began to relax, softening with each advance and releasing as he pulled back.

Until he brushed a spot inside that made her tighten around him involuntarily as blue stars bloomed behind her eyelids.

"Wait," Mason ground out, grappling for control. "Don't move."

He looked down at Charlotte, her lovely legs open for him.

She was so damn beautiful. She felt so damn good.

And it had been so damn long.

Held in her wet, taut heat, feeling like not just her sex, but also her entire being molded itself around him, he wanted to give everything he had promised. To stun her with pleasures she would relive endlessly when committing them to words in her novel.

He'd been arrogant. Cocky, even. Thinking his experience would give him the upper hand in this scenario.

With her wondering gaze aimed up at him, he realized just how wrong he'd been. The half-shy, half-wanton way she looked at him stoked some hidden ember of his soul. Stripping him of all bravado. Laying him bare. He wasn't Mason Kane, or a billionaire playboy, or any of the versions of himself he'd carefully curated and presented to the world.

He was only a man inside a woman who heated and haunted him. Who worshipped and ruled him with the simple gift of her body.

She was going to be the death of him.

And he had never longed more for obliteration.

Seeming to feel his hesitation, Charlotte carefully pushed herself up on one elbow and placed a hand on his stomach, tensed with the effort of holding himself back. Curious fingers traveled the bony ridge of his sternum, up the channel between his pectoral muscles, helpfully distracting him. Reeling him back from the brink.

He wished he could crawl into her head at moments like these. To see himself from her vantage. Surely he hadn't earned the frank adoration radiating from her like the sun's own rays.

When Mason trusted himself again, he guided her back to the mattress and draped one of her legs over his hip. He nudged the other wide as he leaned down to wind her wet braid around his fist before planting it next to her neck.

And he moved in her.

Long, deliberate strokes at an angle that yielded the deepest parts of her. Charlotte met him blow for blow, rocking her hips into him, urging him on. And on. And on.

The end built within him like the waves in the sea beyond, gathering, gathering, ready to sweep in. To cover all.

Their mouths merged, lips fusing, tongues sparring, drinking each other's moans like heady young wine, never, ever getting enough.

She tightened around him on a whimper as buried.

himself to the hilt, pulling a deep, guttural groan from the very depth of his soul. Rhythmic pulses at the root of his cock overtook him, pleasure too vast for his body to contain flooding from his scalp to the soles of his feet. Heedless, helpless, he threw back his head and roared with the release.

Panting and spent, he collapsed to his elbows over her. Their bellies were glued together by sweat, his nose against the silk of her neck, her damp braid pressed to his cheek. They stayed until their breathing slowed, the warm breeze cooling their passion-heated skin.

He rolled to his side, greedily examining her body for every sign of their joining before it faded.

Her lips were kiss-swollen. Her small, perfect breasts sex-flushed and rosy. Her legs slick with sweat, dappled by the temporary tattoos of his hipbones, his fingers, his mouth.

As if drawn by the force of his eyes on her, Charlotte moved to face him. The pale specter of her hand floated over to his face, pushing a sweat-dampened lock out of his eyes.

"Hi," he said.

"Hi." A satiated Cheshire cat grin spread across her face.

"You better not smile at anyone else like that." Mason reached across the space between them to brush his thumb over the corner of her mouth. "I might get jealous."

The smile deepened. "I've already been jealous."

A trickle of alarm leaked through him. "Of who?"

"Everyone," she said. "But especially that time we hosted the customer appreciation event at the sand dunes during SupplySide West."

Mason dipped into his infamously unreliable memory, sifting like a miner panning for gold. "The one where Samuel had his accident?"

She nodded, her cheek rustling against the lounger's fabric. "First Samuel had asked me to make sure you and Arlie flew together to Willow Creek for that promotional shoot. Then he asked me to make sure your rooms were next to each other in the block at the Fairmont. And for the dune buggy event, he said to put you two up together even though it was supposed to be broken into teams pairing customers with Kane Foods employees."

"But my room wasn't next to Arlie's at the Fairmont. And the flight you had booked for me to Napa was canceled." Charlotte's eyes darted away just as realization crystallized in his mind. "You *knew what Samuel was trying to do*?"

"Since when has Samuel ever taken an interest in any-one's travel plans?" she asked. "Unless it was to track who had been buying first-class tickets more often than economy. Anyway, the dune buggy part I couldn't help, because he was actually going to be in attendance, but when I saw the way you and Arlie were all over each other during the cocktail hour portion, I was afraid that his plan to tempt you into making a play for Arlie had worked after all." Her warm fingertips barely grazed his.

"And that made you jealous?" He wanted to hear her say it. To think of her there, watching them together.

"Extremely," she said. "Of course, the way she took off running when Samuel rolled his buggy made me feel a whole lot better, and she ended up telling me ev-erything anyway. I still can't believe that Samuel was capable of going to such elaborate lengths to get you pushed out of the company."

Given their tumultuous history, Mason had been somewhat less surprised.

Charlotte nestled closer to him, escaped strands of hair fluttering in the breeze as she covered his hand with hers. "I'm really sorry that happened to you, Mason. I can't imagine how I would feel if Jamie had done something like that."

Though Mason had since reconciled with his twin, her words brought back the pain of Samuel's betrayal like a tent stake through his heart. "It's not like either of us ever made things easy on each other—"

"No," she interrupted, cutting him off. "To plot against your own sibling like that is fucked up. I don't care what the circumstances were, and if no one else will say it, I will."

An odd mix of affection and arousal swelled through him. "I don't think I've ever heard you say that word before."

"Clearly you've never read my books."

Beginning at her shoulder, Mason ran a hand down the dune of her rib cage where it dipped into her waist and swelled into her hip. "Clearly I need to."

Unfazed by his obvious attempt at distraction, she lifted her hand from his and placed it on his jaw. "Samuel was lucky that you stepped in for him like that. When your father found out about him and Arlie and tried to get Samuel to resign? The fact that you would be willing to step down as CMO if your brother was forced out. That was really selfless of you. Just in case no one has said that, either."

It hadn't been, though.

Not really.

This was something he had only recently admitted to himself. Part of him had hoped his father *wouldn't* back down. That Mason and Marlowe would have to make good on their promise to leave Kane Foods in solidarity if their brother was made to.

The cards had landed in Samuel's favor, and Mason remained exactly where he was.

Stuck.

The thought widened and deepened the nexus of pain until Mason could no longer bear it. He needed to keep this part of his life—of himself—separate from the woman who seemed to determined to pull it to his surface. To take away its sting.

Because to let her do that, was dangerous.

Feelings couldn't be part of their future, so keeping them out of the present was mandatory.

Using a leg lock it had taken months to master, he quickly rolled her beneath him, eliciting a startled yelp.

"With all due respect," he said, pushing his quickening erection into her hip, "Samuel is the last thing I want to talk about right now."

With a knowing grin, Charlotte mimed locking her lips and throwing away the key.

Ten

Charlotte paced the length of her suite, the click of her heels alternately amplified and muffled by the varying surfaces of polished marble and plush rugs. She checked the grandmother clock on the fireplace mantel for the seventy-third time.

Eight twenty p.m.

Mason was twenty minutes late.

After their poolside encounter and a decadent three-hour nap, they'd sipped champagne from a miraculously refreshed ice bucket, then ravenously devoured a poolside picnic of fresh seafood, crusty bread drizzled with green olive oil, tapenade and thick smears of creamy goat cheese.

They'd parted ways at four, with Mason promising to come collect her at eight for an evening he insisted would be "a surprise." His lone instruction had been to wear whichever she liked of the dresses they had acquired at Retrospect.

She had selected the pale green vintage Halston with a snug sweetheart bodice, scooped back and long silk skirt that swirled about her ankles as she walked the length of her balcony and assured herself she had nothing to be worried about.

At least, not where Mason was concerned.

In the four hours since she'd seen him, she'd caught up on the surprisingly few work emails she'd received, had a phone call with Jamie—nothing to report other than Mom was doing fine and David was creeping back into his DMs—and spent some time on her balcony working on her book.

When her eyes had crossed and her brain hurt, she slipped into the tub and took her time soaking, shaving, then applying her makeup and arranging her hair into a softly waved half updo.

It had been while she was zipping herself into her gown that the next text came.

You don't know him like I do.

Madison had been added to the list of suspects. Retaliation for the way Mason had hustled her out of the office before making a beeline for Charlotte's desk.

She might still have been waiting outside the building when Charlotte had left early.

Then again, it could be Bentley Drake, who could just as easily have seen her leave with Mason the night of the fight.

She shook her head as if to rid it of these spiraling, unhelpful thoughts.

Eight twenty-three p.m.

Irritation gave way to anger as she realized she didn't even know where Mason's room was. And what would she find if she showed up at his door?

Would he be on the phone with *her*?

A knock at her door set her heart leaping into her throat.

Checking herself in the full-length mirror, she drew in a deep breath and banished the scowl from her face.

"Come in," she called.

The heavy wood swung inward, and there he was, devastatingly handsome in a black-on-black tuxedo and a familiar self-deprecating expression of apology slipping straight off his face when he saw her.

His lips opened in a single, whispered syllable. *"Wow."*

She made a show of glancing at the clock, unwilling to let him charm his way out of this one. Life-changing, soul-twisting, back-blowing sex or no.

"I didn't realize the French Riviera also operated on Kane standard time."

"Mea culpa." He hung his head in exaggerated shame as he crossed the room to her. "There were a few last-minute details I had to put in place for tonight."

Once upon a time, she would have considered herself—perhaps incorrectly—a fairly decent judge of sincerity. God knew she had seen enough of its opposite to know the difference.

Mason followed none of the patterns she relied upon when employing her bullshit detector. No subtle facial tics or averting of the eyes. No fidgeting or performative fussing.

The longer she spent with him, the harder he was to read.

"You look…stunning." His hand slid around to her bare back, pulling her toward him, fingers trailing down her spine. His tan was deeper in this light, casting his eyes in an even more verdant hue. Had he spent some of the four hours they'd been apart being worshipped by the Mediterranean sun?

"So do you." She tugged the sharp lapels of his coal-black shirt and smoothed a hand over the slim, silky obsidian tie.

"I spent a lot of time picking that, you know." His voice was husky and low.

"Well, it matches your suit perfectly."

"It's not my suit I was trying to match." With a swift flick, he untucked the tie from his vest and captured her hand.

She swallowed hard as he gently wound it once around her pale wrist.

"Perfect." He looked at her from beneath lowered brows. "It's the width that's difficult to calculate. But we don't need to worry about that until later."

The cloud of lust darkening his expression passed as quickly as it had come, and he was once again the casual, jovial man she knew.

"Shall we?" He stepped to the side and offered her his arm.

She took it, pausing to put her phone in the small, beaded ivory evening bag Kassidy had insisted Charlotte take as a loaner.

Given Mason's penchant for driving, she was surprised to see an old black Packard limousine and uniformed chauffeur waiting for them in the drive.

"I don't want to have to pay attention to anything but you tonight," Mason explained, noting her bemused expression.

His words almost made her feel guilty for the amount of time she'd spent telling herself stories about him this past hour.

But then again, wasn't that what she did best?

Moments later, they were ensconced in the limousine's cabin of buttery leather and inlaid wood, winding their way down the hillside, the moon playing hide-and-seek among trees swaying in the night breeze. The air was dim and close, lit only by the small, glowing bulbs over the polished minibar on Mason's side.

Slouched on the seat, long legs splayed out in front of him, he was largely silent during the twenty-minute drive, staring out the window at the clusters of flickering lights and the night-black water reflecting shingles of moonlight.

Which did precious little to help her unease.

At last, the car pulled up in front of a sprawling, colonnaded building.

Diamants didn't look like a casino. At least not the casinos in Atlantic City Charlotte had visited with her parents on occasion—nicotine-yellowed and smoke-hazed, redolent with flashing lights, drink-stained carpets and dull-eyed stares glazed blue by slot machines.

No, the building Mason escorted her into was more like an opera house. Polished wood bars and high ceilings, thick carpets and chandeliers. It was uncrowded but well attended, each of the rooms bearing a dazzling assortment of beautifully dressed people. Men in bespoke suits and tuxedos. Women dripping diamonds and trailing expensive perfume.

She followed him into a room with a large, green felt–covered rectangular table and roulette wheel at its center.

A murmur of conversation rose from the participants gathered around its edges, swelling into a chorus of elated and frustrated shouts as the small white ball dropped into a slot that displeased as many people as it delighted.

"Will you be joining the table, Mr. Kane?"

A man with an elegant Swiss accent, pristine white shirt and black vest had appeared at Mason's elbow.

"Yes, Henri." He smiled at Charlotte. "And so will my guest."

"Oh, no," she protested, speaking as much to Henri as Mason. "I'd prefer just to watch."

Mason leaned close, his breath tickling her ear. "The only way I'm not going to lose my mind with you in that dress is if you let me teach you roulette. Two seats," he said, turning his attention back to the attendant.

They were shown to two tall leather chairs halfway down the table on the side facing the door. No sooner had they sat than a stunningly beautiful woman in a chic black sheath appeared to take their drink order.

"The usual?" Mason asked and, liking the familiarity between them this suggested to anyone who might care to listen, Charlotte nodded.

The drinks were placed before them in record time,

and Mason dropped a purple chip on the tray, earning him a grateful smile from their server.

With the bourbon beginning to loosen her joints and the roulette wheel ticking out a lulling melody at regular intervals, she surrendered herself to Mason's eager explanation, words like *croupier* and *odds* and *French bet* and *en plein* sifting themselves into her consciousness.

"Essentially, it's all about odds." He was coming to the end now, glancing at the table and placing chips in several black squares.

Charlotte looked up to find the woman across the table from them flicking a sly glance at Mason for the third time since they'd sat down. Her dark hair was wound into an elegant chignon, her tight, white dress revealing several inches of smooth cleavage and showing off her flawless tawny skin to perfect effect.

"What if I just want to hold on to what I have?" She swirled the amber bourbon around the perfectly clear cube of ice in her glass.

"Where's the fun in that?" He arched an eyebrow at her, grinning as he took a sip of his scotch.

"In not giving away something you can't get back?" she said, willing him to understand the deeper meaning in her words.

"That's why you never put on the table more than you can afford to lose."

It was impossible to read in his expression whether he was only talking about roulette.

Charlotte watched as he slid his own bet onto the table and made another on her behalf.

"No more bets," the croupier announced, the small white ball bouncing in the blurring wheel.

Only when the anticipatory gleam vanished from Mason's eyes did she notice the man hovering near her shoulder.

Tall and elegant in a polished, continental way, he had dark, neat, close-cropped hair silvering attractively at the temples and an amused slant to his mouth. His fastidious tuxedo was the color of fresh cream, the expensive jacket interrupted by the perfect triangle of black handkerchief in the breast pocket.

Mason went pallid beneath his tan.

"Mason Kane," the man said with a polite incline of his head. "What an unexpected pleasure."

She couldn't quite place the accent. Austrian, perhaps?

"Niklas." Mason sipped his drink, keeping his eyes fixed on the table.

The man stayed, looking at Charlotte expectantly.

When Mason didn't introduce her, the man offered her his hand. "Niklas Hafner," he said.

"Charlotte Westbrook," she said, a little flustered when he leaned over and brushed his lips over her knuckles in a totally outmoded but nostalgically chivalrous gesture.

"Utterly charmed." Niklas released her hand and lifted a frosted martini glass to his lips. "Will you be staying all evening?" he asked, directing the question to Mason.

"No." The word was short and sharp.

She looked at Mason, noting how his posture had changed. Shoulders hunched, hands fisted on the edge of the table.

"Now, that is a shame," Niklas tutted. "Does that you

mean you won't be bringing your lovely date to our *private* table?"

"Correct," Mason said tightly.

"A pity," he said, giving Charlotte a long, lingering look. "Speaking of…that reminds me. How is Madison? Her company has been *sorely* missed at our little *gatherings* these many months."

Madison.

An acidic mix of worry and suspicion began to congeal in Charlotte's gut. Not only had Mason been here with Madison, her presence had been memorable enough to bear mentioning.

"You have five seconds to leave, Niklas." Warning honed Mason's voice to a dangerous, flinty edge.

"Are you sure I can't urge you to reconsider? Miss Westbrook would be such a intriguing addition to the evening's entertainments—"

There was a blur of black, and Niklas's head snapped backward, the clear liquid in his glass making a slow-motion arc through the air before splashing across Charlotte's lap. She leaped out of her chair, her hands flying first to her dress, then to her mouth as she saw Niklas crumpling to the ground and Mason kneeling over him, fist suspended above his upturned face.

"Mason, *stop*!" she cried.

Dark-suited security guards descended and pulled Mason off the other man. "You stay *the fuck* away from her," he growled, his eyes wild and teeth bared, nearly succeeding in throwing one of the guards off.

A man wearing an earpiece helped Niklas to his feet. "Our apologies, Mr. Hafner."

Niklas sniffed and dabbed at the red smear below

his patrician nose. "Quite unnecessary. I would, however, be glad of some help with my jacket." He glanced down at it sheepishly, as if it were stained with wine rather than blood.

"Of course, sir."

Niklas quickly handed his coat off before turning to Mason with a mocking little bow. "Until next time."

The chatter resumed.

Charlotte's eyes swam with tears of humiliation, her cheeks burning and her mouth metallic with adrenaline. She spun on her heel and ran toward the front door, ignoring Mason's shouts in her wake.

She needed to get out.

To get away.

Once outside, she kicked off her heels, picking them up by the straps and running barefoot on the grass until she reach an old cobblestone path that led down toward the water.

"Charlotte!"

Mason's voice floated down to her from the top of the hill, but she ignored him, needing to put as much distance as possible between her and all those gilded, grinning, smugly superior smiles.

"Charlotte, wait!"

Panting, she reached the edge of the overlook, a waist-high brick wall preventing her from fleeing any farther.

The old city sprawled below, proceeding at uneven steps and slopes.

She planted her hands on the rough stone, cooling from the night but still holding a hint of the day's heat. Mason's shoes were gritty on the path behind her, his breathing hard.

"What was Niklas talking about?" Charlotte didn't turn to look at him. "The private table. The gatherings. The *entertainment*?"

His exhale was gusty. Defeated. He walked up beside her, leaving a respectful distance as he looked out over the night sky. "Madison introduced me to Niklas when I was going through a particularly self-destructive phase before I joined The League. We ended up traveling with his group of friends to Monte Carlo, Malta. Anywhere where hedonism was the order of the day. Within that circle, monogamy was somewhat of an outmoded concept. Only, I lost interest in their proclivity for sexual musical chairs after the first few times. An unforgivable offense, apparently."

Charlotte felt like a brick had been dropped on her chest. Deep down, some part of her acknowledged that she had already suspected this. Had read it in the way Niklas's eyes had moved over her body.

"Why would you bring me here?" she demanded, turning to him. "When you've been here with *her*? And other women as well?"

Mason stalked toward her with the lean, predatory grace she had witnessed while he was in the ring. A hot wall of anger radiated through the black fabric of his shirt.

"Why should it matter who I brought here or why if all you want out of this are details for your book?"

The back of her neck bristled with irritation.

"And if all *you* wanted was to show me how billionaires really live, then why would it matter if Niklas propositioned me or not?" She gave him a bitter laugh. "Those are the kinds of games you like to play, right?"

He backed her against the wall, the stones biting into her hips through the thin silk fabric of her gown.

"Not with *you*." His voice shook as he folded his fingers around her upper arms. Charlotte blinked up at him, startled to her very depths by the raw emotion in his emerald eyes. He leaned in and pressed his forehead against hers.

She stood completely still, afraid that the slightest move might break the spell that held them in this rare moment. The ocean's rush and the wind sighing through the trees were the only sounds.

"You're right, Charlotte," he said quietly.

"About what?" she whispered.

"You don't belong around people like them. People like *me*." Scalding self-loathing twisted the last word into something ugly and shameful. He drew back and searched her face.

"When I saw you in the crowd at The League fight that night, you took my breath away. I had never seen you look so…so *alive*. And then afterward, at my penthouse, the way you were so desperate to capture every detail because you'd never tasted anything like that bourbon, never spent time in a place like that purely for your own pleasure, I just…wanted to give you *more*. Give you anything and everything that put that light in your eyes."

"You did, Mason." Charlotte hugged her arms to her torso. "No one has ever done anything this thoughtful, or generous, or—"

"That makes it fucking worse!" He pulled away from her, creating space for his impassioned words. "It kills me that you don't realize just how beautiful and kind and intelligent and amazing you are. That you don't understand that men so much better than me would cheerfully murder each other to set the entire world at your feet. Instead, you allow people like my father to treat you like shit, and you come back every morning and let him do it again, because you *have* to. Because you have to support and care for your mother while useless wastrels like me who don't deserve *shit* are handed anything we want on a silver platter. It's a sick goddamn joke."

With a gentle hand on his shoulder, Charlotte turned him to face her.

She studied his rumpled hair and his furrowed brow, at the fine, thin line over his eyebrow already knitting itself together, the faintest hint of the fading bruise at the corner of his mouth. These signs that he'd chosen to unleash his wrath on the very group he both hated and belonged to. To beat and be beaten by it.

"*You* are not a joke, Mason," she said. "And you didn't get to choose your family any more than I got to choose mine. But you do get to choose how you respond to it. Hitting people isn't going to make your pain theirs any more than numbing it away or distracting yourself will help you cope in the long run."

A small, sad smile shaped his lips.

"What do you do to cope?"

Charlotte looked to the lights dancing over the darkened water. "I escape."

Mason closed the distance between them. "Please," he said, brushing his fingers over her cheekbone. "Don't escape from me."

His mouth lowered to hers, lips melding, tongues tangling in a passionate dance as his hands slid downward.

A deep rumble vibrated through his chest as he discovered she was pantyless beneath her gown. She'd meant to reveal this to him at some mundane moment in an evening that had proved to be anything but.

"Come with me." He took her hand as Charlotte stepped back into her shoes and swiftly walked her back up the hill. In mere moments, he had gathered their things from the casino coat check and joined her in the back seat of the waiting limo.

In that close, dim shared space, Charlotte faced a man ill suited to her in every possible way. If anything, what had unfolded over the course of the last hour irrevocably cemented that fact in her mind. Every single thing he'd said about his life, about the way he'd lived, was true.

And yet, rehearsing this fact to herself failed to dampen the fuse Mason had lit within her body. Sizzling as it traveled down her nerve endings, daring her to let it explode.

Resisting him felt like swimming against an undertow. Fighting a force more vast and powerful than the moonlit sea sparkling beyond the car's tinted windows.

What would be left if she yielded to its pull?

Charlotte didn't know.

Just as she didn't know how to stop herself from melting into him even while the one-word warning blared like a foghorn over and over inside her head.

Wrong. Wrong. Wrong.

How could this man be so wrong, but feel so right?

Eleven

The ride to Château du Ciel was a blur.

All the while, Mason kissed her.

Kissed her until the rush of her own pulse drowned out the chorus of her racing thoughts.

Kissed her as she had never been kissed before: by a man who thoroughly knew the art. A man who knew how to make kisses seem not like the preamble to something more, but as the end, the means and the method all at once. His hands anchored in her hair, stroking her neck, her collarbone, her arms and shoulders, but nowhere else.

And it drove her absolutely, completely mad with want.

When they at last pulled up in front of the villa, her knees wobbled as she headed up the front steps.

Mason lifted her into his arms, carrying her over the

threshold like it was their honeymoon, across the foyer, up the grand staircase and straight to her suite. Almost a direct enactment of the very scene she'd been hoping for upon their initial arrival.

She reached down and opened the door, and he shouldered them through, depositing her on the tall four-poster bed.

He took several steps backward, shrugged out of his jacket and tossed it onto a chaise longue as he stepped out of his shoes and pulled off his socks. Loosening his tie, he left it draped over the collar of his shirt.

With a little ripple of anticipation, Charlotte remembered his earlier words about selecting it carefully. He walked over to the fireplace and flipped on the gas flames, a golden glow bathing him. At the side table, he withdrew a lighter from the drawer and touched it to each of the points of the candelabra, repeating the process until every candle in her suite was lit.

Her breath was shallow and labored as she grappled for control of her senses.

He kept his eyes on hers, lifting her ankle in his hand and unlatching the strap on her high-heeled sandal, removing it from her foot like Prince Charming in reverse. Just when she expected him to turn his attention to the other, he lifted her bare foot to his lips and kissed the arch before propping it on his shoulder. Only then did he retrieve the other foot and repeat the process, placing it not over his shoulder but against the hard length in his pants.

His eyelids lowered incrementally as Charlotte pushed the sole of her foot against him, exploring.

Mason unbuttoned his shirt and stripped it off, followed by his belt and then his tuxedo pants. And then he was standing before her in black boxer briefs, the black silk tie still slung around his neck.

The candlelight played over the planes and angles of his body with a worshipful reverence, dancing in his eyes. He caught the hem of her dress and began sliding it slowly, slowly up her calves and over her knees, pausing when he had it halfway up her thighs.

Grasping both her ankles, Mason rolled her face-down on the bed before easing her off the edge. He unzipped the dress to let it pool at her feet.

Charlotte felt the tie. Cool and silky as he trailed it down her spine and lower, following the curve to her wet heat.

"Put your hands on the bedpost," he ordered.

However sophisticated she was trying to appear up to this point, she couldn't resist a glance back to see if he was serious.

He was.

Very.

Obediently, she swiveled to place her hands against the smooth, polished wood. Mason leaned over her, his torso warm against her back as he quickly secured her wrists to the post with a few expert loops and tugs of the tie.

"Mmm," he hummed appreciatively. "I like you like this, Miss Westbrook."

The use of the formal appellation in this setting kindled a spark low in her belly.

She heard the muffled sound of him removing his boxers and felt his foot between hers, sliding her legs apart. He gripped her hips, his hair-roughened thighs hard against hers as he bent his knees to slide his arousal against but not inside her.

Charlotte moaned when the head of his cock nudged her throbbing bud only to feel him slide back to do it again and again.

Fingers trailed up the ladder of her ribs, and he filled his hands with her breasts, catching her taut, sensitive nipples between his index and middle fingers and squeezing.

Mason made an instrument of her, sent vibrating chords of pleasure singing through her entire body with a single pluck.

"You're so wet," he growled, quickening his pace against her. "Do you have any idea how much I want to be inside you? How it's been driving me absolutely insane all night?"

"I want that, too," she panted. Her knuckles whitened as her grip on the post tightened, her knees weakening slightly at the admission.

"Then come for me, Charlotte."

He changed the angle of his hips, redoubling the friction as he gently pinched her nipples.

The sweet clench of release detonated at her middle, and she would have collapsed had Mason not held her steady. When she again had control of her own legs, he quickly undid the knotted tie and released her hands, lifting her onto the bed and crawling onto the covers next to her.

She rolled on her side to look at him, willing her brain to burn this image of him into her memory for all time. If these days were all she would ever know of a man like him, of pleasure like this, she could accept it as long as she could close her eyes and visit him in the darkness behind her lids.

Her fingers traced the edges of the wolf's muzzle on his pectoral muscle in the guttering light.

"Remus," she whispered. "I remember that myth. Raised by a she wolf. Killed by his twin brother Romulus who went on to found the city of Rome."

Finding the ridge between his pectorals, she traced it down his abdominals and over the dangerous line that narrowed at his groin into the small, dark patch of hair over his sleek, powerful sex.

"Remus Pax. The twin who makes peace." The spark of recognition flared in his eyes.

"Don't look at me like that," he rasped, his voice tight and husky.

She explored him with her fingers, marveling at how it could be so silky, hot and hard all at once. "Why not?"

"Because one day you'll stop." His stomach tensed as she caught the pearly bead of moisture at its tip and slicked it over him. She moved to try to bring her mouth to him, but he caught her under the arms and pulled her onto his lap, her knees straddling his hips and her breasts level with his face.

She didn't answer him. *Couldn't* answer him. Didn't want to make promises neither of them knew if they would be able to keep.

Mason traced the curve of her jaw, the side of her neck, the ridge of her collarbone and down to her sternum, only stopping when his hand was over her heart.

It beat wildly beneath his palm as their eyes locked.

Charlotte placed her hand over his and guided it

down to the place that ached and wept for him. "I want you."

His lids lowered over eyes dancing with reflected flames. "Then take me."

Mason saw the nervousness flicker across her features.

Judging by the way her thighs tightened when he pulled her on top of him, he suspected that she wasn't particularly practiced in this position.

Which was exactly why he wanted it.

Their eyes were locked in challenge. Her delicate jaw set in a look of determination that utterly gutted him.

Reaching behind her, she gripped his erection and lifted it from his stomach, dipping backward to spear herself. Inch by maddening inch until she drove him all. The. Way. Home.

He hissed a breath between clenched teeth at the exquisite sweetness of being inside her.

"Jesus," he groaned, fingertips dimpling the soft flesh of her hips.

With him completely sheathed inside her, she wrapped her hands behind his neck and drew him up until they were face-to-face.

Mason was undone by the shocking intimacy of it, being this close to her, sharing breath and locking eyes while she began to move. She rocked slowly at first, her face lifted toward the ceiling, her glorious hair spilling down her back.

"That's it," he urged, adding gentle pressure and angling his hips to deepen their contact.

"Unnh." The vibration of her moan began at her mouth and ended at his cock.

Their bodies were slicked with sweat, torsos sliding against one another, her ass gliding over his hips and upper thighs.

A slow, sweaty screw.

Tugging a handful of her hair back to expose the pale column of her throat, he feasted on her fragrant skin, feeling the pulse of her jugular against his lips, nipping at the underside of her jaw, tasting every inch of her.

"You're so beautiful," he whispered, flicking his tongue into the shell of her ear. "And you feel so fucking good."

"So…do you." Her words came in pants.

Mason reached beneath her arms to hook his hands over her shoulders, driving himself deeper. Her head fell backward, the ends of her hair sweeping his thighs as she released a throaty cry.

Fingers laced behind his neck, her chin descended and they were once again facing each other with this new depth of pleasure plumbed and building between them.

Their gazes met and held.

Charlotte wasn't just looking at him. She was *seeing* him.

And he saw her.

It was raw and real. Completely unrehearsed and unfiltered. So unlike his overly performative encounters where the faces and bodies of both participants were always arranged into the most flattering of expressions and angles for each other's delectation.

Where connection only occurred on the physical

level and the act was a game itself, the rules well understood by both parties.

Now, with her face bathed in an intimate glow, candlelight reflected in her eyes, a part of himself he'd never felt in thousands of such nights began to wake.

Not the wildly beating muscle within the cage of his ribs, but something deeper and more central to his being. A place radiating an all-consuming tenderness. A fierce, urgent need to protect her, to defend her, to feed her, to do anything and everything he could to keep pain and sadness from stealing away the pure ecstatic wonder written on her face.

This was the one luxury he'd never permitted himself.

To be trusted with the care of another person.

He rolled her beneath him, suddenly hungry to have every part of his body touching every part of hers. To marry his chest to her breasts, to glue together the taut, sweat-slicked skin of their stomachs, to feel her thighs with his. She gazed up at him, her parted lips proving too much of a temptation for him to resist despite having to relinquish their eye contact for him to claim them.

Charlotte surprised him with the fierceness of her response, her hips surging upward as she wrapped her ankles around his calves. He moved within her slowly, leaving nothing unexplored, breaking the fusion of their mouths only to drink in the sight of her.

"Charlotte." His throat constricted, damming up all he couldn't bring himself to say.

Her hand softly molded to his jaw, the careful tenderness of the gesture threatening to split his already-aching heart straight down the middle.

The heat they had been slowly kindling together ate through their bodies like wildfire, burning all reason in its wake. Their breath came faster as their joining became more demanding, neither of them holding back.

He felt a darkly delicious pain as she scored his back with her fingernails, her teeth sinking into his shoulder as he felt her tightening around him.

An answering tightness curled low in his belly.

When he said her name this time, it was a warning.

Charlotte hooked her ankles behind his back, driving him deeper than he'd even thought possible.

"Fuck." He growled as his release ripped through every part of him like lightning, seeking ground, finding it at his core in endless spasms.

He looked down at her, utterly undone by her brazen expression of seductress's pride.

Knowing what she had done to him and loving that she had.

He collapsed onto his side on the bed without disentangling their bodies.

A rosy flush bloomed beneath the fresh scattering of freckles their time by the pool had caused. Her lips were swollen and glistening, tilted upward in a contented smile, her eyes as remote and lovely as galaxies seen through a telescopic lens.

He ran a single lock of her hair between his fingers, sliding all the way to the end. "We have a problem," he said.

"What's that?" Her words were loose and languid.

He picked up another lock of her hair and repeated the process.

"I'm never not going to want you now."

More than once over the past couple days, he'd found himself picturing their return to work the following Monday. Her behind her desk and him in his office, passing by each other with polite greetings and trying to not think about her face in the candlelight and her skin under his fingertips.

The scenario he had promised.

A promise he was now breaking with this admission.

She blinked, her lids lifting as she looked at him intently. "What does that mean?"

Mason patted his sternum in invitation. "We'll figure it out."

Charlotte hesitated a beat before resting her cheek and ear against his pectoral muscle, the crown of her head tucked under his chin and her breasts molded against the side of his rib cage. She reached one arm across his torso, anchoring it on his opposite hip and curling her leg around his.

He stroked her bare back, his fingers following the gentle dip of her spine and following it down to the elegant dimples at the top of her hips.

The night breeze moved over them, drying their sweat and making the candle flames dance.

They talked.

Trading questions and stories until the candles died and dawn crept in through the billowing curtains. And as the light faded from gray to gold, they found each other again. Charlotte's back against his torso and his fingers gently gripping her hips, the conversation never stopping as he took her from behind.

At last, they slept, a few hours in sex-tangled sheets,

waking when a knock at the door reminded Mason that he'd ordered breakfast be brought to them at 10:00 a.m.

Mason yawned and rose to his elbow. "That will be room service."

An adorably grumpy expression crumpled her delicate features as she moaned and folded the pillow over her face. He wondered if Charlotte would be a morning person if she didn't have to arrive for a job by 7:30 a.m. every day.

He peeled the covers back and walked to the bathroom, where he shrugged into one of the thick terrycloth robes provided before opening the suite door.

A cart draped with a white tablecloth and laden with silver-domed dishes and a gleaming coffeepot was parked outside. Tall, condensation-fogged carafes of fresh-squeezed orange and cantaloupe juice beckoned his eye. The aromas of crisp bacon and freshly baked bread wafted up to his nostrils, and Mason became aware that he was suddenly ravenously hungry.

Elbowing the door open, he rolled the trolley inside, parking it next to the doors leading out to the balcony.

Charlotte pushed herself out of bed and padded toward the bathroom with the bedsheet tucked around her. This act of self-consciousness after everything they'd done together produced an oxytocin-fueled stab of tenderness he didn't even bother fighting off. She emerged several moments later in a bathrobe and her hair tamed into a long, thick braid, joining him at the bistro table overlooking the ocean. The day had taken on a distinctly Mediterranean palette of dusty greens, spicy terra-cotta reds and tranquil topaz blues.

Forgoing her usual shyness, she tucked into the food

with an enthusiasm that met his own, helping herself to flaky croissants with butter and fresh berry preserves, bacon, and a fat wedge of quiche with Gruyère, country ham and mushrooms.

"Not exactly your typical breakfast for the region," Mason said, pouring out the coffee. "But the staff are very accommodating when I'm in town."

"Everything is wonderful," she mumbled around a mouthful of croissant and glob of glossy red clinging to one corner of her lip. Her eyebrows shot up in alarm when she caught his bemused expression. "What?" she asked.

He leaned across the table and kissed the corner of her mouth, stealing the jam with a quick flick of his tongue. "Not a thing."

She dabbed at the spot with her starched white napkin and resumed eating, but with slightly less gusto.

"Don't," he said. "I like watching you enjoy yourself like that."

"Like what?" she asked, pouring cream into her coffee from the small silver pitcher.

"Like a woman who isn't afraid of her appetites."

Her cheeks flushed predictably as she poured cantaloupe juice into one of the glasses. "I've always wanted to try this."

"We can try anything and everything you've ever wanted."

This garnered him a well-earned eye roll as she shook her head. "*Is* there anything we haven't tried?"

He felt a wicked grin stretching across his face as he mentally conjured up a few of his personal favorites. "Absolutely. But if there's anything you'd like to do between the times I'm ruining you for all other men, I'm certainly open to that as well." He took a lusty bite of his own croissant, relishing the delicate buttery flakes and sweet preserves.

Charlotte's fork paused halfway to her mouth, a bite of quiche quivering on the tines. "What kinds of things?"

"We could play around on the Jet Skis, or take a boat out on the water for a sunset cruise, or pack a picnic for the beach."

"How about all of the above?"

He grinned at her contagious enthusiasm. "You do realize we have all week?"

"I'm sure we'll have no problem filling the time." She looked at him from beneath her lashes, and just like that, the vixen had returned.

Hunger sated, they both leaned back in their chairs, her bare feet resting atop his. "Shower?" he suggested.

"Sure," she said.

They rose and walked to the sitting area, where he consulted the phone he had set next to hers on the wireless charger.

"You go ahead," she said, perching on a chair next to the table. "I'll be right in. I'm just going to check my messages really quick."

He raised a censorious brow at her. "Not your work messages, I hope."

"Promise." Charlotte drew an X over her left breast with her finger.

In the gleaming bathroom, Mason hung his robe on a silver hook beside the large glass-and-marble shower stall and turned on the full-body-massage jet. He sank into the bracing spray, relishing the feel of the steaming water moving over his sweat-salted skin.

Head tipped back, he let the jets hit him full in the face and beat against his overexerted muscles. The exhaustion had just begun to leach from his body when alarm rose in him like mercury at the echo of Charlotte's concerned voice from the other room.

"What do you mean, you can't find her?"

Twelve

We can't find Mom.

Charlotte had never liked how crisis had a way of transforming every aspect of the world around her.

The daylight paled. The air thickened. Ordinary objects became absurd props forever attached to the visual stimuli of the initial shock.

"What do you mean, you can't find her?" The words sounded unreal, spoken from some source outside herself.

"Gail and I took her to the farmers market." Jamie's voice was shot through with panic and produced a sick knot of dread low in her gut. "They were looking at some organic produce when Mom said she needed to go to the restroom. Gail found a store that had one. When Mom didn't come out, Gail went in and checked, and she was gone. Apparently there was a door to the bathroom that opened to the outside."

A bitter mix of bile and adrenaline soured on her tongue. She was staring at the wood grain of the table when, inches from her gaze, Mason's phone screen lit up with a text message.

The name gave her already frazzled nerves a jolt. Madison.

She saw the message without trying, her eyes flicking automatically to the partial text shown on the lock screen.

I'm sure you did, handsome! Can't wait to hear all about the charity case—

Her pulse sped further as she realized this read like a *reply*. Stunned, Charlotte wrested her attention violently away from Mason's screen.

"Where are you now?" she asked her brother.

"Driving around in my car. I dropped Gail off at hers so she could look, too. I've already called the police. They're sending a unit over."

"How long?" she asked. "How long have you guys been looking for her?"

"About an hour."

"An *hour*?" she stammered. "Why didn't you call me?"

A beat of silence. "Because I was hoping she would just turn up in one of the stalls and I wouldn't have to worry you."

When you're too far away to help was the unspoken ending to that sentence.

Guilt lanced her as she pictured herself, sex-rumpled and self-satisfied, gorging on croissants and sipping

French coffee while her brother frantically searched the streets for their missing mother.

Mason appeared in the doorway, his narrow hips swathed with a towel, his hair dripping above a face creased by concern.

"I'm going to let you go, Charlotte," Jamie said. "The police just got here."

"Okay," she said. "Call me as soon as you talk to them."

"I will. I love you."

"I love you, too." Charlotte disconnected and set her phone on the table. The sound of her own heartbeat throbbed in her burning ears.

"What is it?" Mason asked. "What's wrong?"

She brushed past him to the large polished wardrobe in the corner, pulling out her suitcase and setting it on the bed before returning to grab fistfuls of the clothes she'd neatly tucked away in the drawers. "I need to leave," she said. "Now."

The wounded look on his face was almost enough to temporarily dislodge the panic crushing her lungs. "Why? What happened?"

"My mother wandered off. My brother has been searching for her for the last hour. He called the police." Her eyes stung as she viciously yanked the lingerie from its hangers, hating how frail and frivolous the fabric felt against her skin. She seethed at the pure, irresponsible uselessness of it. At herself for having let Jamie talk her into buying it.

"Hey." Mason quickly crossed the room and attempted to pull her into a hug. Charlotte ducked from his outstretched arms and went back to her phone, pulling up her travel app and quickly punching in the search details. "There's a 2:35 p.m. flight that gets into Philadelphia at seven," she said, squinting through the glasses she had jammed onto her face, aware she was speaking mostly to herself. "If I can get to the Nice airport within an hour and a half, I should be able to make it work."

"Charlotte." Mason's hands landed on her shoulders, turning her to look at him. The scents of his naked skin and herbaceous soap hijacked senses she needed to dedicate to the task at hand.

She backed away from him. "Is there a local agency that offers airport service?"

"Charlotte." He said it more firmly this time, the sound of it so similar to Parker Kane's you-will-listen-to-me tone that it made her irrationally angry.

"What?" she snapped.

"Think about this for just a minute. Don't you think you should at least give it a couple hours to see if they find her?"

The soundness of his logic resonated instantly, of course, and was all the more irritated for it.

With sagging shoulders, she turned toward the full-length mirror. In it, she saw the ghostly pale color of her flat, expressionless face, her red-rimmed eyes standing out against her blanched cheeks. She looked ridiculous, standing there in the fluffy white robe. A poor excuse for the pampered spa-goer in the ads for upscale resorts she frequently scoffed at.

Mason sidled slowly up to her, meeting her eyes in the mirror. "It's going to be okay."

"No!" She whirled on him, the thunderheads within her breaking open in a sudden, unstoppable rush. "It's not."

Mason blinked at her, shocked by her sudden fury. "I just meant—"

"You meant that for you, everything always *is* okay," she accused, quickly adding, "In the kind of family where I was raised, things *aren't* always okay. I left my mother there with my brother, who isn't used to caring for her, and now she's missing, and if anything happened to her, I am never going to forgive myself for being so selfish and irresponsible. Coming here was a mistake."

He took a step back. "This was *not* your fault, Charlotte," he said. "And just because something bad happened the one instance when you actually took some time for yourself does *not* mean it was a mistake."

A heavy sigh escaped her. She stalked over to the bed and leaned against it, allowing the mattress to bear a measure of her weight. "You offered to show me the inside of this world, and you have, and I'm grateful for that. But if there's one thing I've learned from being inside, it's that there's a reason I'm on the outside. This is my reality, Mason. I don't have the luxury of assuming I can just sit back and figure things out. My life is medical bills and caregivers and emergencies and canceled plans. The mistake was thinking I had any hope of convincing myself otherwise."

Mason walked over to the bed and seated himself on the same edge but several feet away. "And I think you're looking for reasons to convince yourself that's true."

"Looking?" she asked incredulously. "I don't have to go looking for anything. The reasons are everywhere. They're in your office, at your vacation rental, at the casino. Hell, they're in *my* phone."

In *his* phone, too. But Charlotte feared that if she so much as breathed the words *charity case*, the tide of tears she was desperately trying to hold back would flood to the surface.

A furrow appeared between his eyebrows, his posture stiffening. "What are you talking about, Charlotte?"

She shoved herself away from the bed and returned with her phone. Opening the screenshots she'd taken of the three separate messages, she pushed it into Mason's hands.

He glanced at the phone and then at her. "What is this?"

"Just read it."

His gaze dropped to the screen, his emerald eyes scanning as he thumbed through the messages. The muscles in his jaw bunched, his mouth flattening into a tight line edged with white. When he spoke, his tone was steely and cold. "Why didn't you tell me about this?"

"Because you're not my partner or my protector and this is not a relationship. It's sneaking around behind your father's back. Rolling the dice."

Mason looked like he'd been sucker punched. There was something so incredibly innocent about the sudden widening of his eyes and the involuntary frown that flickered across his mouth that, for a moment, she almost felt a spasm of regret.

Because deep down they both knew it was true.

"I'm sorry, Mason," she said. "I don't mean to seem ungrateful. Everything you've arranged, all the care you've taken in trying to show me beautiful places and give me beautiful experiences. I really do appreciate it. But your world is never going to be my world. And I'm not sophisticated enough to play pretend."

"Who's pretending?" Mason handed the phone back to her. "Why won't you let me be here for you?"

"Because what good will that do?" Charlotte pushed herself away from the bed and paced the length of the floor-to-ceiling windows opposite the balcony. "I've spent years learning how to handle things on my own. What happens when I start relying on someone else and I'm even worse off when that support goes away?"

He was thoughtful for a moment, staring out over that ludicrously beautiful shoreline. When he looked at her, his eyes were a darker shade than usual, seeming to borrow some of the blue. "There *are* no guarantees in life, Charlotte. Not for any of us. But I'm here. Now."

She *wanted* to go to him. To let herself collapse in the circle of his arms. To let him shore her up, even if only for a season. But her feet remained rooted to the spot, bound by a steely thread of self-preservation.

"I'm sorry, Mason." Her voice hitched. "But you're a bet I can't afford to lose."

He pressed his lips together and nodded. A utilitarian gesture. Brutally casual in its application. As if he'd just been told that a flight had been canceled or his luggage lost in transit.

The shrill jangle of her phone split the yawning silence between them. Yanking it from the pocket of her robe to answer, she could tell immediately by Jamie's greeting that the news wasn't good.

Jamie sounded shaken and winded. "We haven't found her yet. I talked to Officer Russo. They're sending as many units as they can spare."

"Slow down," Charlotte urged. "Take a deep breath."

When she glanced up, she saw that Mason had silently slipped out of the suite.

Jamie's exhale crackled through the phone's speaker. "I just don't understand how she could... I was being so..."

"This is not your fault. Or Gail's. You didn't know there was a second door out of the bathroom. You guys were in a really populated area. She has a medical alert bracelet. Someone is going to see her and call."

"I'm so sorry." His words were thick with regret. "The last thing I wanted is to ruin your trip."

"No," she insisted. "Don't do that. This could have happened to me just as easily."

"But it didn't," her brother said.

"I'm coming home, Jamie." She had saved this information for last precisely because she knew how it would be received.

"No," he insisted. "Please. At least give it a couple hours."

"It's not just Mom," she assured him.

"What happened? Do I need to hurt him?"

Even through her worry, Charlotte felt a pang of fondness. The idea of her sensitive, artistic brother attempting to inflict pain on Mason Kane was as endearing as it was utterly ridiculous.

"No," Charlotte said. "It was just...unsustainable."

It being that fleeting, addictive, drugging, top-of-the-world high she'd felt until reality had come crashing through the paper walls of this fantasy she'd allowed herself to build.

"Shit," Jamie broke in. "That's Officer Russo on the other line. Can I call you back?"

"You better," she said.

He did after a few minutes, but with no developments to report.

Charlotte decided to take a quick shower, keeping a ritual she usually lingered over as brutally short as possible, as if denying herself any kind of pleasure at a time like this.

When she exited the bathroom in a towel, Mason was there.

Fully clothed in a familiar uniform of charcoal-gray slacks and tailored violet shirt, he sat at the desk with his broad back facing her.

She cleared her throat, painfully aware of her dishabille in the face of his expertly styled presence.

Charlotte didn't know what she had been hoping to see on his face but knew instantly this wasn't it.

All business, Mason stared at the screen of his phone. "Can you be ready to fly in forty-five minutes?"

The question paired with his carefully conscripted manner made him resemble Samuel more closely than Charlotte had ever witnessed in her years at Kane Foods.

"I can," she said, her stomach at once sick and glad.

"Good." He rose from the chair and marched toward the door. "I'll meet you in the foyer." His hand was poised over the polished handle when she surprised herself by speaking his name.

He turned slightly to look over his shoulder.

"Thank you," she said.

Mason pushed the door open and left.

Thirteen

This had officially been the longest day in Mason's entire life.

Which was saying something, considering just how many times during his formal schooling and college years, when forced to sit through lectures and exams, he had felt like entire swarms of locusts were eating his brain.

Never had the interior of a private jet seemed so claustrophobic.

Never had the mere offer of a bourbon made him want to crawl out of his own skin.

Haunted by memories of their first flight together, he sat several rows back from Charlotte and on the other side of the aisle, lest he launch himself into the chair next to hers.

After they'd reached cruising altitude, he'd taken up

a station on the couch farthest from her and done his best to erase the memory of the sweet scent of her hair as she'd wheeled past him in the entryway of Château du Ciel.

If silence was what she wanted, he could give her that, at least as he had failed to deliver on any other end of their bargain.

Against his will, he relived his confusion at her chilly shift when he'd come out of the shower. Panic, he could have understand. Worry, too.

While he understood her urgent impulse to leave, he had been utterly, infuriatingly perplexed by her sudden rejection.

No.

Perplexed wasn't the right word.

Hurt.

He'd been hurt, and it scraped at his pride to admit it.

He had ached—physically ached—with the need to annihilate the space between them. To hold her. To thumb the salty tears from her cheeks and tell her that everything would be all right.

To be *able* to make everything all right.

The particular outcome wasn't in the realm of his control, but he did have some contacts from his extracurricular activities who possessed skill sets he thought might come in especially useful in the current situation.

In the spate of time Charlotte had talked with her brother and quickly readied herself for their flight at the villa, Mason had called in every favor he was owed not only in Philadelphia, but also in the tristate area and beyond.

And they were many.

He had been obsessively checking his phone until he'd had to flip it into airplane mode for their initial ascent, relieved when he could free himself from his seat, crack open his laptop and get to work.

His stomach flipped when he saw the email at the top of his inbox once he'd successfully connected to Wi-Fi. From *variable78@protonmail.net*, one of his contacts looking for Charlotte's mother. No subject line. Target located. Disoriented but otherwise stable. Transported to Einstein Medical Center. Police will contact the brother ASAP. Safe flight.

The email had been sent roughly ten minutes ago.

Then he heard Charlotte gasp.

"ASAP," indeed. Well done, *Variable*.

She shot out of her seat and whirled around to face him, nearly upending her laptop in her haste. "They found her!"

A lifetime of behind-the-scenes machinations and fibs both large and small had left him amply qualified to quickly arrange his features into something approximating surprise.

"They did?" he asked, mirroring her breathless exuberance.

"Jamie messaged me on Facebook." Her face flushed with excitement. "The police just called and told him she's at Einstein Medical Center. He's on his way over there now."

"Is she okay?" Already knowing the answer, Mason tried to inject just the right amount of concern into his voice.

She nodded rapidly, her eyes filling with tears as she pressed a hand to her twisting mouth. "She's all right. A little scraped up and dehydrated, Jamie said. He's going to let me know when he's been able to talk to a doctor." Her voice broke on the last word, and it took every ounce of strength Mason had to prevent himself from pulling her into his arms. From assuming she wanted that kind of comfort from him.

Instead, he stood, but only to offer up the box of tissues from the table next to the couch. "Are *you* okay?" he asked.

Charlotte pulled out a tissue and dabbed at her cheeks, lifting her glasses to swipe it beneath her red-rimmed eyes.

"This has just been…a lot." She sniffled and offered him a watery smile.

"I can't even begin to imagine." He set the box down and folded his arms across his chest, unsure of whether to sit or stand. Feeling like a stranger in his own body. Just wanting to do or say whatever it was that would keep her here, looking at him. Talking with him.

She seemed equally uncomfortable, at least. Standing there, chewing the inside of her cheek, dressed in a loose, flowing white tunic blouse, jeans and sandals. Though he hadn't seen everything she'd packed, he'd seen enough of it to know she'd likely opted for the most purposefully platonic and practical outfit she could assemble.

Damn him, the vision of her determinedly examining and rejecting the other options was so deeply endearing it only served to enflame him further. He wanted to reach up and release her hair from the haphazard bun at the base of her neck. To cup her clean-scrubbed face and drink from the deep caramel depths of her eyes.

"Well," she said, effectively cutting through the thickening tension. "I better stay plugged in."

"Of course," he said. "We'll have to make a fuel stop in Zurich, but we should still be wheels down by 5:00 p.m."

When she'd returned to her seat, Mason shifted his attention to the second item on his list of concerns.

The mysterious texts Charlotte had received.

After sending another round of emails, he reluctantly dug into the mound of work-related tasks he'd been neglecting.

The remaining hours passed at a maddeningly sluggish rate, the sound of Charlotte tapping away at her laptop filling much of them. Mason dozed off briefly, waking with a kink in his neck and a powerful thirst. After splashing his face with water in the larger-than-average restroom closet, he returned to the cabin and found a scotch and water waiting on the table in front of the couch.

Thinking—or hoping, perhaps—it might have been Charlotte who ordered it on his behalf, he walked on stiff legs toward the front of the cabin, where she had remained stationed throughout the flight.

He found her slumped against the shaded window, eyes closed, dark lashes feathering her cheeks, mouth soft in sleep.

Her laptop was open on the tray in front of her, the blue-white glow reflected in the lenses of her glasses, which were cocked at a precarious angle, having been pinned between her head and the cabin wall. As carefully as he could, Mason lifted them from her face, folding them before placing them in the cup holder on the armrest. Noting the prickles of gooseflesh on her forearms, he slipped down the aisle and came back with a blanket.

As he leaned in to drape it over her, his eye caught on a line of text preceding the flickering cursor on the document open on the screen.

I'm sure you did, handsome! Can't wait to hear all about the charity case—

A jolt of dread shot down his spine.

Madison's text.

He hadn't seen it until after he'd left Charlotte's room to pack his own things.

When had Charlotte she seen it?

He mentally rewound their day, carrying them back over the ocean, down to the private airfield at Nice, driving them in reverse all the way back to the villa, mentally unpacking their bags, not stopping until he could find the last moment when she had looked at him and smiled.

Before the shower?

His phone had sat on the charger, but she couldn't have opened it without the pass code. Which meant she must have seen the text—or part of it, at least—flash on his locked screen *while* she was talking to her brother about her mother being missing.

Unbidden, his eyes moved down the page.

A sick, hot wave turned her stomach at the words crawling across his screen like angry, spiny insects as she realized this wasn't just a message. It was a reply.

In fact, it had been. An answer to Madison's initial text, which had been an extremely compromising picture of the two of them with the question Bored of Daddy's secretary yet?

I meant what I said in my office, Madison had been his reply.

Part of him wanted to shake Charlotte awake that very second. To make her read the entire exchange and show her his side. But then the next line in her manuscript leaped out at him.

When the initial rush of anger and humiliation subsided, she began to recognize an eerie calm descending in her mind. The kind of rare quiet she only felt standing alone in a world hushed by an unexpected snow. It was a mercy, really. The exact wake-up call she needed. After only a day spent with him, it had merely scalded her heart. But if she let herself fall for him any harder, it would have incinerated her entire being.

If all love was a gamble, he was more than she could afford to lose.

Mason's thoughts raced as he stalked back to the sofa and sat down hard, draining half his glass in a single swallow.

Was this how Charlotte truly felt?

Had she been falling for him? Or was he allowing his own unexpected feelings cloud his judgment of a purely fictional reimagining of their time together? Had she also found what was supposed to be a purely temporary and transactional fling developing into something more?

Resting his elbows on his knees, he raked his hands through his hair. As Charlotte had pointed out, there were multiple factors at play.

Such as the texts she'd received.

He'd stealthily sent them to himself while she'd been packing and deleted the evidence from her phone history instantly afterward. He hadn't yet heard back from the contact he'd forwarded them to for investigation, shortly after Charlotte's mother had been found, but was confident his answer would come.

Hours later, they finally touched down and rolled to a stop at Philadelphia International. Mason rose and stretched, waiting until Charlotte had gathered her things before making his way to the jet's exit door.

She looked at him curiously when she noticed both Mason's Aston and a sleek black Audi parked on the tarmac, a driver waiting expectantly by the open trunk.

"I thought you'd like to get to the hospital directly," he said by way of explanation. "I'm afraid I have a few things to attend to."

And by *things* he meant the text he had received from Marlowe shortly after he once again had cell reception.

SOS Come to the house as soon as you land.

Exhaustion thick as wet concrete poured over his shoulders as he wondered what fresh fuckery lay in store.

They faced each other on the flat expanse of cement, the city hazy in the distance.

"Let me know how things go?" he asked.

"I will." Charlotte hesitated, her body swaying forward, then quickly back on her heels before she walked to the car.

Mason watched the red taillights shrink into dots as they drove away, wondering if she had looked back at him through the deeply tinted windows.

He didn't even remember driving back to Fair Weather Hall, the Kane family's sprawling neo-Georgian monstrosity on a seventy-five-acre estate outside the city. His great grandfather had built it to give the other titans of the confection industry the bird after they'd mocked his embrace of new chocolate processing machinery. A move that had ultimately driven his competitors to bankruptcy.

Scarcely had Mason's loafer crossed the threshold when he was hustled into the library by Marlowe, who quickly closed the double doors behind them. Samuel was seated in one of the Louis XV Bergère armchairs scattered throughout the cavernous space.

"What. The fuck. Were you thinking?" asked Mason's eternally serious, compulsively uptight twin. He wore pressed slacks and a dress shirt and looked annoyingly fresh despite its being nearly evening on a Sunday.

Mason should have known the library would be Samuel's woodshed of choice. Until the present moment, he had always liked this space. The place where his mother had colluded in building blanket forts against their father's wishes when he was out of town. Mason had always found the contrast especially delicious. Frolicking all day long in pajamas amid the priceless paintings, turning the uncomfortable decorator-selected couches into pirate ships.

"I'm not sure I know what you mean." The phrase

was hackneyed but also his go-to response ever since he was a child first starting to get into trouble.

"Bullshit." The word was venom on Marlowe's lips. Her platinum bob shimmered around the elegant angles of her face as she folded her arms across her chest. "You flew Charlotte, on a private jet, to Château du Ciel in Côte d'Azur."

"You've gotten even more sophisticated at the black ops financial snooping." He fixed her with a sarcastic grin. "Been dipping into that private flight tracking technology to predict potential mergers again, little sister?"

Marlowe winced like a cat avoiding unwanted petting. "You know I hate it when you call me that."

"Her point is, you made it painfully obvious." Samuel began his lecture with the baleful tones of disappointment he'd honed to perfection over the years.

"As opposed to that time I had to bail your ass out when you and Arlie ended up on the front page of a local gossip rag?" Mason asked.

Arlie Banks appeared in the doorway from the adjoining study as if summoned by the mention of her name. "Can I get anyone a drink?"

"Vodka tonic," Marlowe said without missing a beat.

"Scotch and water," Mason followed.

"And for you, darling?" Arlie tucked a lock of wheat-blond hair behind her ear, a diamond roughly the size of an ice cube glittering from her finger.

"I'll have an old-fashioned, love," Samuel said.

In prior days, Mason would have rolled his eyes at the instantly gentle and dreamy expression that transformed his brother's face. But now, witnessing it made him feel pierced and lonely. He couldn't stop himself from drifting back to the memory of Charlotte beneath the billowing canopy of the bed, gazing at him with a poignant mix of adoration and wonder.

"You got it." Arlie cast a worshipful glance in Samuel's direction before disappearing into the study.

"You know you two are actively disgusting?" Marlowe perched on the extreme edge of a chaise longue, and for the first time he could remember, Mason wondered if he had ever seen his sister truly relaxed. Her eyes, the same pale blue as their father's, fixed on Samuel, and Mason was grateful not to be the center of attention. If only for a moment.

"I'm sorry," Samuel said, sounding not sorry at all. "Is it the bored mutual toleration between you and Neil what I'm supposed to be aiming for?"

"My fiancé is hardly our chief concern at present." A blankly offended look on her face, their sister drew herself to the full pinnacle of cool, offended hauteur. A move their mother had frequently teased Marlowe for during her moody teenage years.

"And I am, I take it?" Mason asked.

"Your unbelievably idiotic and irresponsible decision to engage in a casual fling with our father's executive assistant is, yes," Marlowe bit back.

"What makes you assume my interest in Charlotte is of a casual nature?" Mason asked. True, it may have started that way, but—

His brother and sister chose precisely this moment to burst into loud, raucous laughter, made all the more irritating by the rarity of its occurrence from either of them.

Mason's phone vibrated in his pocket. Thinking it might be Charlotte, he pulled it out and checked the screen, heart pounding in his ears when he saw the contents of the text. If he could have, he would reached through the phone and smacked a kiss straight on the lips of his bookie's second cousin's nephew, who spent great spates of time cruising conspiracy theories on the dark web when he wasn't hacking cellular networks.

Before he could interrupt his siblings to share what he'd learned, the library door swung open.

Their father paused on the threshold, commanding their full attention.

He was undeniably elegant in gray slacks and a midnight blue smoking jacket; Parker Kane was the only man Mason had ever known who could wear one without looking ironic. His pewter hair had been wet-combed and his mirror-polished shoes traded for the cashmere-lined, buttery leather slippers he wore when at home.

"I fail to see the humor," he said, every word echoing like a gunshot, "in your having flagrantly disregarded my only inviolable rule."

Mason, Marlowe and Samuel exchanged the lightning-quick glances they'd perfected in childhood, both of Mason's siblings telegraphing they hadn't been the ones to tell their father.

Parker Kane strolled forward, hands fastened behind his back and Neil at his heels.

Marlowe's fiancé followed their father into the library like some overbred lapdog, breaking off to stand behind Marlowe, who stiffened at the hand he placed on her shoulder. God, how Mason wanted to wipe the smug, knowing smile off his exfoliated face.

With his fist, preferably.

They waited, as they always had, for their father to take his station before the windows, his back to them.

"When Neil informed me that he'd seen you and Miss Westbrook exiting the family wing of the executive floor together, I dismissed his suspicions outright," he said, managing to make this sound like a gift Mason hadn't deserved. "But based on further information he's shared with me, it seems there is merit to his allegations after all."

Mason paced closer to the chaise, if for no other reason than Neil tended to shrink like a salted slug in his physical proximity.

"While I've always appreciated your sense of pageantry, Father, and Neil's quest to become the literal dictionary definition of a lickspittle, I'm just going to save us all some time by confirming there's a shit ton of merit to his suspicions, and that's pretty much exactly what I came here to tell you."

Samuel's and Marlowe's mouths dropped open in unison as their father spun to face him.

"Frankly, I don't know what additional information Neil has provided you, and I don't especially care. Apart from the fact that it probably came from confidential financial records only Marlowe is supposed to have access to."

Marlowe cast a questioning look up at Neil, whose eyes failed to meet hers.

"What I'd like to know," Mason continued, "is whether

Neil told you he's been sending Charlotte bizarre text messages from a variety of cell phone numbers?"

Neil's face and neck went ghost white.

Marlowe stood, arms crossed over her chest as she faced him. "Neil?"

He made no answer.

Mason turned to address him directly. "Ratting me out to my father, I could understand, because it's what I've come to expect from you. But targeting Charlotte? There is absolutely no motive there that doesn't have its roots in you being a creepy fuck."

Neil opened his mouth as if to speak, but Mason rolled on.

"'I know where you were last night. Why aren't you at home? You don't know him like I do,'" he said, reciting words that had been burned into his brain. "Kinda makes you sound jealous. Like maybe the whole reason you're coming after me is because of *her*."

Neil glanced frantically between Marlowe and the Kane patriarch, one of whom looked stricken, the other ready to strike.

"Is this true, Neil?" The question came from his father, who pinned Marlowe's fiancé with a stare that had proved as effective as sodium pentothal in evincing the truth from just about every human save Mason.

"Charlotte is an asset to Kane Foods. You know Mason's habits better than anyone." Here, Neil aimed a beseeching look at Marlowe. "I only wanted to prevent her from making a terrible mistake."

"See, that holds up right until you realize the only way you would have known she came home with me last Thursday would be that you either have some way of tracking her phone or you followed her to my fight and waited to watch her leave. Honestly, I'm not sure which is skeevier."

"Fight?" Samuel leaned forward with keen interest.

"Long story," Mason said. "Point is, I'm happy to accept the consequences of my actions. All I'm asking is that Neil does, too."

Marlowe resembled nothing so much as an ice sculpture, so cold, stiff and ethereally beautiful that it came as a shock when she spoke. "I think you should leave, Neil."

Neil blinked at her, his overmanicured brows drawing toward each other in exasperation. "You have to understand—"

"No," Samuel said, rising from his chair and crossing the Persian rug to stand next to Mason. "She doesn't."

To have his twin at his side, united in protection of their sister and mutual contempt for Neil, balmed a place Mason hadn't known needed soothing.

Neil flung a last-ditch look at their father, who had turned back to the sprawling lawn, neat as a putting green, hands again folded behind his back.

Faced with a sight that had withered better men, Neil uttered a disgusted grunt and stalked from the room.

His sister was notoriously hard to read, but having known her since the day she arrived on the planet, Mason saw the flash of pain in her face. There and gone as quickly, replaced by her usual placid veneer.

She was fine.

Marlowe was *always* fine.

Moments later, Arlie returned with their drinks, carrying them to the expansive buffet table, where she set down the ornate silver tray.

Mason couldn't help but stare at it.

For the metaphor it represented.

The uncanny privilege of their upbringing. The ways it had shaped and warped them all.

"I hope you don't mind," Arlie said, lifting an extra cut-crystal tumbler of amber liquid from the tray. "But I thought you might like a drink as well."

To Mason's absolute and utter shock, he realized she was addressing his father.

When he failed to turn, Arlie started across the carpet toward him, ignoring Samuel's emphatic if subtle signals to stop.

"Here you are," she said brightly, holding out the drink.

Parker's glacial eyes slowly moved over her, his face assembling into the disapproving but resigned expression usually reserved for a stray you've failed to discourage from following you home.

His hand closed over the glass.

In his peripheral vision, Mason saw his siblings exhale a breath they'd been collectively holding.

Arlie beamed a smile at him as she glided toward Samuel.

Their father stared into the drink as if consulting an oracle. "What are your intentions, Mason?"

Accepting his scotch from Arlie, he sipped at the drink to steel his resolve. "I'm formally resigning as the chief marketing officer of Kane Foods International."

At his side, Samuel broke into a hacking cough, having aspirated a mouthful of his old fashioned.

"Oh, Mason," their father said in a patronizing tone, "if this is your idea of a grand romantic gesture—"

"It's not," he interrupted, saying the words while adrenaline still sang through his veins. "I'm not sure if you noticed, but I've been absolutely miserable for years."

His father chuffed in disbelief. Soft, shuffling steps brought him from the windows over to the tawny Biedermeier settee, where he seated himself. "You've certainly done an effective job of disguising this fact."

"No." Marlowe set her glass on the side table and folded her hands in her lap. "He hasn't. Not for a long time."

Samuel shifted beside him.

The velvet of their father's smoking jacket rustled as he drew in a deep breath and let it out slowly.

"I've been very patient, Mason," he said. "Tolerant. Turning a blind eye to your exploits and preserving your good name when necessary. But to abandon your duties? To turn your back on your family legacy? This, I cannot abide."

Mason walked to the sitting area and sank into a chair across from the settee.

"That's not what I'm doing," he said. "I know my reputation suggests otherwise, but I've given this a lot of thought. My stepping down is the best possible thing I can do both for the family and the company. Samuel is the heart and soul of this operation and always has been. With Marlowe's eyes on the money and a new chief marketing officer who's actually passionate about the role, my leaving will be beneficial to operations in every way."

His father's head tilted at analytical angle. "This sounds very much like the excuses you offered grow-

ing up, when you gave up your many hobbies and pursuits once you discovered they required perseverance,
hard work and dedication."

"The difference, Father, is that this isn't a hobby.
It's a career. And it's one I never wanted. It's what *you*
wanted for me."

Words he had swallowed. Buried. Fought and gam-
bled and burned away. Here they were, out in the room.
The world.

"And yet," his father said, running a finger along the
razor-sharp crease in his slacks, "you've had no issue
enjoying the perquisites of your position."

"You're absolutely right," Mason agreed. "In fact,
I've deliberately exploited them as often as possible."

This earned him a mumble of agreement from Samuel, who had seated himself in the large, leather chair
where he had spent so many summers, Arlie perched
on the arm next to him.

"Deliberately wasting resources is nothing to brag
about, Mason." That his father—a man who routinely
purchased cases of wine that cost more than a house in
the suburbs—said this with a straight face struck Mason
as strangely hilarious.

"I'm not bragging," Mason said. "I'm admitting. My
point is, I don't want the kind of life I can only tolerate
by running away from it."

Because that was, after all, exactly what he'd been
doing, however much he'd tried to convince himself
otherwise. Seeking pleasure. Seeking distraction. He'd
found both in Charlotte's arms, but something else as
well.

The truth.

About himself. About the dreams he'd once had. About the future he wanted and what he had to do to build it.

"If you were to leave Kane Foods," his father said, crossing one leg over the other, "exactly what is it you plan to do with your life?"

Encouraged by his father's use of the conditional, Mason sat back in his chair.

"I have absolutely no idea," he admitted. "But I'd like to find out."

"Ludicrous." Swiftly rising, his father dismissed the notion with a regal sweep of his palm. "Embarking on some kind of journey to *find yourself.*" He pronounced these words with a derisive sneer. "You know who you are. You are a *Kane.*"

Mason stood to face him, hands balled into fists at his side. "Who I am is your son," he said, his voice quaking with barely restrained emotion. "Not your employee, your property or your legacy."

Thick silence suspended them like insects in amber.

"You always did have your mother's flair for the dramatic." His father strolled to a bookcase as if this was the only reason he'd risen. "I'll humor your request for the time being. But I suspect this little rebellion of yours will be short-lived."

Mason felt like a physical weight had been lifted from him.

"But as we're discussing practical matters, what are your intentions regarding Miss Westbrook?"

"Charlotte," Mason said. "Her name is Charlotte. And not that it's any of your business, since my no longer being with the company invalidates your *rule*, but my intention is to be a part of her life in any way she'll let me."

This, like his decision to resign, had solidified with every mile he drove toward his family's estate. Each tick of the odometer that carried them farther apart.

"What happens when things blow up?" Samuel's question came with a larger measure of alarm than Mason would have expected. "Do you have any idea how much Charlotte actually *does* at Kane Foods?"

"I do," Mason said. "And while I can appreciate your panic at losing the woman who picks out the holidays gifts for your entire client list and gets your alterations for free because your tailor is basically in love with her, she's drowning."

"Drowning?" Marlowe's pale brow furrowed.

Their father leaned an elbow against the shelves, giving them his profile as he massaged the bridge of his nose. "Perhaps you'd like to tell me what you want so I can bring this endlessly tedious conversation to a close and retire for the evening."

Mason summarized his demands as efficiently as he could. Once he'd given his gruff assent, their father swept from the library, leaving the three Kane siblings and Arlie behind.

Samuel waited for several beats before breaking the silence. "May I ask how Charlotte feels about the prospect of being in a committed relationship with you?"

Clearing his throat, Mason retrieved his drink. "She might have raised a few valid concerns."

Arlie, who had witnessed the proceedings in a careful silence, laced her hand with Samuel's. "What are you going to do?" she asked Mason.

A deep, centering certainty grew within him as he met each of their eyes. "Everything I can."

Marlowe set her drink down on the side table next to her with a determined clunk and stood up.

"Tell us how we can help."

Fourteen

Charlotte rolled her carry-on bag up the narrow path to the front porch, feeling weary and dull and about a thousand years old. Jamie held the screen door open and pulled her into a hug as soon as they'd stepped inside. He blinked his shining eyes when he released her, the smudges of shadow beneath them making him look older than his twenty-two years.

They had both reluctantly agreed to come home and grab at least a few hours of sleep when the doctor informed them that she'd prefer to keep their mother overnight due to her underlying conditions.

"Beer?" Jamie asked, ambling toward the kitchen.

Charlotte parked her rolling bag in the hall and hung her garment bag in the closet before stepping out of her shoes. "Sure," she said.

He opened the fridge and pulled out two bottles, popping the tops off and handing one to her.

They migrated to the living room and sat down on the sofa side by side, legs lazily splayed out before them.

Jamie lifted his beer in a silent toast. "Please tell me you managed to have at least some fun in the whopping forty-eight hours you were gone."

She clinked her bottle with his. "I did," she said.

"But..." He trailed off.

"But do we really have to do this now?" she asked, her shoulders sagging. "I'm completely exhausted and mostly brain-dead and don't know that I can give an intelligent summary."

"How about a basic recap?"

She sipped her beer and sighed, grateful for the cool flavor of roasted grain on her tongue. "I just can't live in that world when everything in mine is...is so real. Real problems. Real consequences. Real—"

"Feelings?" Jamie arched a brow at her, the corner of his mouth curled up in a knowing grin.

She opened her mouth to protest, but he held up a hand to shush her. "I know you. I know your face. I know your voice. And I know when Mason Kane was standing in our living room, you were happier than I've seen you in years. That's real, too."

A single hot tear slide down her cheek. Exhausted as she was, the truth of her brother's words pierced straight to the heart of her.

Charlotte had already known this. She had been trying *not* to know it for most of their brief excursion.

It had always been real for her.

The kindness and warmth he'd shown her from her first day with Kane Foods.

Every mocking smile behind his father's back.

The ways large and small he'd made her life bearable without knowing it.

"Let's get you to bed," Jamie said, clearly aware she'd reached the end of her emotional line. Helping her up from the couch, he steered her toward her room and turned down the covers before pecking her on the cheek.

"Night, Charlie."

"Night, James," she yawned before falling into bed.

The following morning, she woke late to the sun streaming golden across her comforter and her phone trilling on her nightstand. Jamie must have come back and set it there sometime after she'd collapsed.

Reluctantly, she rolled over and slid her glasses on before squinting at the screen. Her stomach did an abrupt death roll when the name swam into focus.

Parker Kane.

She sat up in bed, pushing her hair away from her face and clearing her throat as if she had any hope of convincing him he hadn't roused her from a dead sleep long after she would normally be at work.

"Good morning," she said, cringing at how foggy she sounded.

"Good morning, Miss Westbrook. Do you have a moment to speak?"

"Of course," she said, wiping her instantly clammy palms on the comforter.

"This is the sort of conversation I would prefer to conduct in person," he said, his resonant voice stiff and formal, "but in light of recent events, I'm afraid I have no choice."

Her heart rate sped to a gallop.

He knew.

About her and Mason and Château du Ciel.

"Miss Westbrook, you are being placed on sabbatical, effective immediately."

A pulsing brown aura rose at the edges of her vision, eating away at the periphery. She opened her mouth to speak, but her tongue felt thick and heavy.

"Until such a time as you have completed the manuscript you're working on and have secured more tenable care circumstances for your mother," he continued.

Charlotte blinked, catching sight of the comical expression of confusion on her face reflected in the mirror above her dresser opposite her bed. "I'm sorry…what?"

It was easily the least curated response she had ever managed in Parker Kane's presence, telephonic or otherwise.

"Surely you don't think I haven't noticed how the division of your efforts between these pursuits and your work at Kane Foods has negatively impacted your performance."

Hot sand filled her throat, effectively choking off any hope of her response.

"Which is why, in addition to retaining your current salary, you will receive an additional stipend. I trust you will use it in order to expedite the two conditions of your sabbatical so that you may return to work at Kane Foods as swiftly as possible."

Trust.

The word burned through her initial relief like an ember through paper.

While Mason had made a lifelong career of carelessly dancing with the truth, Charlotte knew that her lie would be a rock in the shoe of her conscience until she set it to rights.

"I can't tell you how much I appreciate such a generous gesture," she said. "But there's something I need tell you before we proceed any further."

The silence that followed went on for an eternity.

She took a deep breath and forged ahead. "When I asked for this week off—"

"Miss Westbrook," he interrupted, "may I give you a piece of unsolicited advice?"

"Of course," she said.

"When someone in a position of power offers you a beneficial arrangement, never assume the arrangement isn't even more beneficial for *them*."

She frowned, attempting to apply this thought to her present circumstances.

"I am a pragmatist, Miss Westbrook," he continued. "While I won't pretend to be pleased that my son chose to completely disregard my imperative regarding romantic attachments in a corporate setting, I recognize the soundness of Mason's logic. You are of your best use to me when you aren't in distress."

Charlotte's mouth dropped open, her eyes wide with shock.

"About Mason—" she began.

"Miss Westbrook," he cut in, "there is no longer a reason to discuss my son or your proximity to him in any regard, as he is no longer an officer of the company."

The buzzing of a thousand cicadas filled her ears. "What?"

"He resigned as chief marketing officer yesterday evening."

Fingers knotted in her blanket, she brought it to her chin. "Resigned?" she repeated. "But—"

"I'm afraid I don't have time to discuss this further at the present moment." His tone was clipped and brusque. Harried. "You should be receiving paperwork regarding the terms of your sabbatical from Kane Foods. Please sign and return it at your earliest convenience."

"Absolutely," she said, embarrassingly overenthusiastic. "Of course. I... I don't know how to begin to thank you."

Parker Kane gave her a grunt of acknowledgment and disconnected the call.

The air conditioner cooled the damp patch where the phone had pressed to her cheek. Dumfounded, she looked up and found Jamie standing in her doorway, his hair sleep-rumpled and his lips curved into a curious frown.

Quickly, she brought him up to speed.

"I'm just so confused," she said finally. "It's like he was complimenting and insulting me at the same time and making me feel he was totally put out but also being amazingly generous? I have no idea what to think."

"Hello." Jamie, who had plopped down on the bed facing her, tapped her lightly on the forehead. "I think it's amazing! No day job while you finish your novel? An extra stipend for Mom's care? What's not to like?"

"The fact that I don't understand *why* Parker Kane decided to do this."

"Let's see." Jamie stroked his chin dramatically. "I wonder *who* could have convinced a notoriously rigid battle axe of a billionaire to do such a generous thing?"

Rolling her eyes, Charlotte batted her brother with

a throw pillow, which he took as an invitation to do the same. They'd fully reverted to their four- and nine-year-old selves when the chime of the doorbell froze them in place.

"Oh my God," Jamie gasped, hands framing his cheeks. "I bet that's him now."

"Right," Charlotte snarked, flopping back on the bed. "Standing outside the bedroom window, holding a stereo playing a Peter Gabriel song."

Getting up from the bed, Jamie grabbed a sundress from her closet and threw it at her. "Get yourself to the bathroom and see what you can do about that mess and I'll buy you some time."

Only then did she realize that her brother was being serious.

"Jamie—" she began to protest.

"Humor me," he insisted.

Charlotte had just managed to wrestle herself into the sundress and had made her way into the bathroom to brush her teeth when Jamie called down the hallway.

"False alarm!"

Did she feel the barest shred of disappointment?

"Who was it?" she called back.

Jamie appeared in the doorway, a curious look on his face and a huge blue envelope in his hands. Her name was written across the front in looping gold script.

"What's that?" she asked.

"Hell if I know." He shrugged, setting it down on the counter.

Her mind flashing back to the anonymous text messages, Charlotte gingerly lifted the creamy envelope, surprised at its heft.

They carried it into the kitchen, where she carefully

slit it with a kitchen knife and withdrew a flat, heavy plaque nearly a sixteenth of an inch thick with a metallic golden border. Her eyes moved quickly over the lines of elegantly engraved script.

The honor of your presence is requested
at a special gathering of The League
on Thursday the 28th of August, 2022,
hosted by Remus Pax.

Standard confidentiality practices
will be enforced.

All proceeds will benefit the
Philadelphia Alzheimer's Research Association.

"Oh. My. God." Jamie's eyes bugged when he lifted it. "This isn't an invitation, it's a charcuterie board—" His words were abruptly hijacked by a gasp, and she knew exactly which part he was reading. "He did *not*!"

"Yeah," she said. "He did." Only when she retrieved the envelope to slide the plate back inside did she discover the note. The small sheet shook in her trembling hands as she unfolded it and read.

Charlotte,
I'd be honored if you would attend, as you're the reason I had this idea in the first place. If not, I would love to see you again, for any reason or none at all.
Yours,
M.

She dropped the note on the table and made a bee-line for the bedroom.

"Where are you going?" Jamie hurried after her.

"I need to see him."

Her brother's features tightened into a polite grimace as he looked her over. "Now?"

"Now." Leaving him in the hallway, she returned to the bathroom, where she brushed her teeth, buffed blush on her cheeks, and brushed her hair back into a quick ponytail at the nape of her neck.

"It's ten o'clock on a Monday, Char," Jamie reminded her. "What exactly are you planning on telling him that can't wait until an hour when cocktails are socially acceptable?"

"These grand gestures, these extravagant acts of kindness." She shook her head while aggressively clearing the sink counter. "How am I even supposed to feel about this?"

Jamie narrowed his eyes and leaned back against the counter. "How *do* you feel about this?"

If only there were a simple answer to that question.

The maelstrom inside her almost defied categorization. Grateful. Confused. Terrified. Hopeful. Overwhelmed. Seen.

She was on the point of answering when a knock at the front door stopped her short. With her heart in her throat and her brother at her heels, Charlotte returned to the front of the house. After disengaging the locks, she swung the door open.

To Mason Kane.

He was dressed for the office: finely cut navy slacks, dove gray shirt and a light blue silk tie with a repeating pattern of minuscule diamond shapes. His dark hair still looked damp in its sculptural waves, his green eyes bright and alert.

She stood frozen, feeling like something that had been dragged out of the laundry hamper by comparison.

"Hi," he said.

"Hi," she repeated mechanically, then seemed to forget that further action was required on her part until she felt a finger poke her sharply in the ribs. "I'm sorry, would you like to come in?"

Releasing the latch on the screen door, she pushed it outward for him to enter.

He stepped past her, the scent of his clean, crisp aftershave mingling with the morning air. "Good morning," he said, spotting Jamie.

"Good morning," Jamie replied. After looking from Charlotte to Mason with an obviousness that nearly made her flinch, he excused himself to make coffee.

Which she suspected meant *start coffee, then stand as close to the dining room door as possible to eavesdrop.*

"Would you like to sit down?" She motioned to the weathered couch beneath the windows looking out on the narrow strip of yard between their duplex and the one next door.

Mason seated himself and waited until she had chosen a spot on the adjacent love seat to speak.

"I was going to wait," he said. "To see if you showed up at the fight. But I realized there are some things I need to say. Whether or not you decide to come to the benefit."

She picked at a loose thread in the couch's fabric. "Okay."

"The truth is, I know that the reason you wanted to come back wasn't just about your mother."

In her stomach, a swarm of butterflies took sudden flight.

"When we were on the flight back, I came over to check on you, and—" he paused as a sheepish smile flickered across his lips "—I read the page you'd written about the text from Madison."

Nervous perspiration bloomed on the back of Charlotte's neck beneath her thick braid.

"I would have assumed the same thing. Given my history." Reaching into the pocket of his shirt, he pulled out his phone. "But I want to show you what the conversation really said."

"You don't have to do that," she insisted.

"I do," he said. "I can't ask you to trust me, Charlotte. I haven't done anything to earn that yet. The best I can do is show you that I'm trying."

The phone felt heavy and expensive in her hand, warm from his body heat. She looked down at the screen and the interwoven text bubbles.

Madison: Tired of daddy's secretary yet?

Mason: We're done, Madison. I meant what I said in my office.

Madison: I'm sure you did, handsome! Can't wait to hear all about the charity case when you get back. Because we both know you'll end up in my bed one way or another.

With her eyes stinging and her face numb, Charlotte handed the phone back to Mason.

"Why didn't you say something? On the plane, after I'd woken up."

"Because you had much more important things on your mind. And because I know that was only one of your reasons. That I would cost you more than you could afford to lose."

Hearing those words parroted back to her stung her with prickling shame. "I didn't mean it like that," she said. "I was upset and overwhelmed, and scared."

"You don't owe me an apology." Mason leaned forward, resting his elbows on his knees. "That's not why I brought it up. It was the way you changed it when you wrote it in your manuscript."

If all love was a gamble, he was more than she could afford to lose. She had felt the truth of those words like roots sunk deep into her very center.

"What do you mean?" she asked.

Mason looked at her. *Really* looked her. "Until you, I had never really known what it felt like to have something I was afraid to lose."

Charlotte could only stare at him. At how different he looked, open and honest and grappling for words. The wonder of his being here, saying these impossible things to her.

"I went into this like the arrogant ass that I am, thinking I could give you something no one ever had and go on with my life. As it turned out, *you* were the one who gave something to me."

"What's that?" she asked.

Mason rose from his sofa and sat down next to her,

taking her hands in his and gazing directly into her eyes. "*You*, Charlotte. You gave me you. Your laugh. Your smile. The way you chew the inside of your cheek when you're thinking and twist your hair when you're nervous. Your shyness and your kind heart. All of it. And if those two days are all of you I'll ever get, I still feel like I've won just to have had you at all. But," he said, gently squeezing her fingers, "if there's any way you'd be willing to try. To let me learn how to be here for you, how to help you, I promise I'll fight to be the kind of man who deserves you."

An ungraceful cross between a hiccough and a sob hitched her chest. "You really want to do this? *Really?*"

Mason squeezed her hands. "Nonfiction. You and me." His handsome face split wide in the wicked grin that had always made her insides feel like melted butter.

"You and me, as in…seeing each other?" she asked.

"I've already seen all I need." He brushed a stray hair that had escaped from its braid. "But we can take this at whatever pace you like."

She drew in a shaky breath and smiled back at him. "And if I'd like to have a dedicated seat in the front row at all your fights and *exclusive*, backstage access afterwards?"

He arched a curious eyebrow at her. "Charlotte Westbrook, are you asking me to be your boyfriend?"

Boyfriend.

How ludicrous this sounded on his lips.

And how completely intoxicating.

"Because I accept." Without warning, he pulled her into his lap and wrapped his arms around her, burying his face in her hair. He dragged in the deep, fierce breath of a man who had just broken the water's surface after meters of swimming upward from the bottom.

"I've been waiting to do this for twenty-seven hours," he mumbled against her ear.

Charlotte closed her eyes and focused on the feeling of his heart beating against her back through the fabric of his shirt. They sat like that, just breathing, just being, until a squeak from the corner of the room caught their attention.

Jamie stood at the dining room door, mug of coffee in one hand and the other fanning his shining eyes.

The rumble of Mason's laugh moved through her, loosening joints she hadn't even known were tight. "Busted."

They reluctantly disentangled themselves, accepting Jamie's offer of coffee.

Through the dancing column of steam rising from her mug, she watched Mason patiently answer her brother's battery of get-to-know-you questions. Including but not limited to: his hobbies, his pet peeves...his shoe size.

"You didn't tell me there were *two*!" being the highlight when Jamie discovered Mason had a twin.

The conversation had progressed to Jamie's desire to open an art gallery and Mason's keen interest in investing in his endeavor when Charlotte's phone rang.

Their mother was ready for discharge from the hospital.

Jamie's effervescent chatter flattened along with his expression and Charlotte knew her brother still felt the sting of guilt.

"You want to go get her together?" she suggested.

"We could stop by that bakery she loves on the way home. Pick up some apple-spice doughnuts?"

It had been a Sunday morning ritual when they were kids, and one meant to anchor them back into some kind of normalcy.

"I'll just throw some clothes on," Jamie said, giving her a grateful smile as he pushed himself up from the couch.

Charlotte collected the coffee mugs and carried them to the kitchen, rinsing each before setting them in the dishwasher. When she returned, Mason and Jamie were standing in the entryway.

"I can drive," Mason offered. "I know you guys had a long night."

"*You* want to go to the hospital?" she asked incredulously.

He slipped an arm around her waist and planted a kiss on her forehead. "Where you go, I go."

With Jamie several paces ahead of them, they locked up and stepped out onto the porch, the late-summer day already warm on their skin as they walked into the midmorning light.

Together.

Epilogue

Acid ate at the pit of Mason's stomach.

Not uncommon before a fight, but this time, it was born of a different source.

Charlotte was late.

Several times, he'd made his way from the locker room down the hall to covertly scan the crowd, searching for the flash of her auburn hair.

And found nothing.

He'd received his last text from her thirty minutes prior. A quick on my way, followed by a string emojis that had momentarily soothed the roiling cauldron in his belly. Charlotte used them so liberally in her messages, they were practically a form of hieroglyphics.

Fondness had faded quickly to concern, then to worry when he didn't receive his requested confirmation of her arrival.

Three times already, he had typed out and deleted various forms of everything okay? messages to check on her progress after her initial ETA had passed.

This was Philadelphia, after all, where gridlock sprang up as randomly as sidewalk weeds and unexpected delays were often endless.

But wouldn't she have sent him a quick running behind if that were the case?

Checking his phone for approximately the hundredth time, he scowled.

Not a peep.

The door to the locker room swung open, and Ralph's gray head appeared in the gap. "You about ready?" he asked.

Mason glanced at the oversize clock on the wall. "Ten more minutes."

From the alarm on his manager's face, you'd have thought he'd been asked to delay a rocket after the launch sequence had already been engaged. "But we've delayed twice already. Don John—"

"Don John and his entire team can eat a bag of dicks." Irritation lanced through him, a welcome distraction. "I'm sponsoring the goddamn fight, Ralph. If I ask them to wait for a month of Sundays, they better fucking well do it. We're not starting without Charlotte."

Charlotte.

Mason found himself steering conversations—bulkily sometimes—just so he could say her name. He had officially become the very thing he had mocked his twin for: a fully ridiculous lovesick fool.

And Mason was absolutely loving every minute of it.

With a quick sideways glance of his baleful eyes, Ralph disappeared.

Just as Mason made to follow him out the door to scan the crowd once more, his phone pinged. He nearly leapt over a towel hamper to get to it.

Relief such as he had never known flooded him in a heady rush when he read the text. I'm here! You got this, baby. A burst of her trademark emojis completed the message.

Standing before the full-length mirror, he slipped in his mouth guard and tested the wrapping on his fists. As was his pre-walk out ritual, he tapped the wolf on his chest three times, kissed his fist and sent it skyward, hoping somewhere, somehow, it reached his mother.

Ralph returned, and Mason gave him the thumbs-up, pushing his way through the door to the fevered cheers surging at the end of the hallway.

He swaggered toward the din and froze when he reached the end.

There, among the sea of faces, he found her. Eyes bright, lips curved in a mysterious grin, whose cause he found when she glanced to her left.

Marlowe, and Samuel, and Arlie.

All there.

All for him.

The reason, no doubt, Charlotte had arrived late. Glowing gratitude moved in and through and over him. Then it was as it had been the first night he'd seen her here, when an entire room of people had been reduced to two.

Just her. Only him.

We. Us.

Such small words, he thought, *but so powerful*. Capable of taking two separate lives and weaving them into a shared story.

And this one was theirs.

* * * * *

Don't miss
Bad Boy with Benefits,
the next story in the Kane Heirs series
by Cynthia St. Aubin!

Available October 2022
from Harlequin Desire.

#2899 BEST MAN RANCHER
The Carsons of Lone Rock • by Maisey Yates
Widow Shelby Sohappy isn't looking for romance, but there's something enticing about rancher Kit Carson, especially now that they're thrown together for their siblings' wedding. As one night together turns into two, can they let go of their past to embrace a future?

#2900 AN EX TO REMEMBER
Texas Cattleman's Club: Ranchers and Rivals
by Jessica Lemmon
After a fall, Aubrey Collins wakes up with amnesia—and believing her ex, rancher Vic Grandin, is her current boyfriend! The best way to help her? Play along! But when the truth comes to light, their second chance may fall apart...

#2901 HOW TO MARRY A BAD BOY
Dynasties: Tech Tycoons • by Shannon McKenna
To help launch her start-up, Eve Seaton accepts an unbelievable offer from playboy CTO Marcus Moss: his connections for her hand in marriage, which will let him keep his family company. But is this deal too good to be true?

#2902 THE COMEBACK HEIR
by Janice Maynard
Home due to tragedy, exes Felicity Vance and Wynn Oliver don't expect to see one another, but Wynn needs a caregiver for the baby niece now entrusted in his care. But when one hot night changes everything, will secrets from their past ruin it all?

#2903 THE PREGNANCY PROPOSAL
Cress Brothers • by Niobia Bryant
Career-driven Montgomery Morgan and partying playboy chef Sean Cress have one fun night together, no-strings...until they discover she's pregnant. Ever the businesswoman, she proposes a marriage deal to keep up appearances. But no amount of paperwork can hide the undeniable passion between them!

#2904 LAST CHANCE REUNION
Nights at the Mahal • by Sophia Singh Sasson
The investor who fashion designer Nisha Chawla is meeting is...her ex, Sameer Singh. He was her first love before everything went wrong, and now he's representing his family's interests. As things heat up, she must hold on to her heart *and* her business...

*Recording studio exec Miles Woodson needs a
showstopping act for his charity talent show,
and R&B superstar Cambria Harding fits the bill.
But when long days working together become steamy
nights, can these opposites make both their passion
project and relationship work?*

Read on for a sneak peek at
What Happens After Hours
by Kianna Alexander

"There's no need to insult me, Cambria. After all, we'll
be seeing a lot of each other over the next two weeks."

"Oh, I see. You're the type that can dish it, but can't
take it. Ain't that something?" she scoffed, then shook her
head. "Let's make a deal—I'll show you the same level
of respect you show me." She grabbed her handbag from
the table. "So remember the next time you open your
mouth, you can expect me to match whatever energy you
throw out."

He watched her, silently surveying the way her glossy lips pursed into a straight line, the defiant tilt of her chin, the challenge in her eyes. She was mesmerizing, disconcerting even. No woman had ever affected him this way before. *She knocks me so off balance, but for some reason, I like it.*

Her lips parted. "Why are you staring at me like that?"

Don't miss what happens next in...
What Happens After Hours
by Kianna Alexander.

Available October 2022 wherever
Harlequin Desire books and ebooks are sold.

Harlequin.com

Love Harlequin romance?

DISCOVER.

Be the first to find out about promotions, news and exclusive content!

Facebook.com/HarlequinBooks

Twitter.com/HarlequinBooks

Instagram.com/HarlequinBooks

Pinterest.com/HarlequinBooks

YouTube.com/HarlequinBooks

ReaderService.com

EXPLORE.

Sign up for the Harlequin e-newsletter and download a free book from any series at **TryHarlequin.com**

CONNECT.

Join our Harlequin community to share your thoughts and connect with other romance readers!
Facebook.com/groups/HarlequinConnection